MEN OF STRAW
NAOMI'S TALE

First Published in Great Britain 2025 by Mirador Publishing

Copyright © 2025 by John Adamson
Artwork Copyright © 2025 by Lucy Christian

All rights reserved. No part of this publication may be reproduced or transmitted, in any form or by any means, without permission of the publishers or author. Excepting brief quotes used in reviews.

First edition: 2025

Any reference to real names and places is purely fictional and are constructs of the author. Any offence the references produce is unintentional and in no way reflects the reality of any locations or people involved.

ISBN: 978-1-917411-33-2

Copyright Information
THE HOLY BIBLE, NEW INTERNATIONAL VERSION®, NIV® Copyright © 1973, 1978, 1984, 2011 by Biblica, Inc.® Used by permission. All rights reserved worldwide.

Men of Straw
Naomi's Tale

John Adamson

ALSO BY THE AUTHOR

THE INFORMER
THE INSIDER
THE DECEIVER

Dedication

This book is dedicated to the memory of two women whose faith stayed strong in the face of every challenge they encountered in life, Joan Ball (1932 – 2024) and Kathleen Adamson (1929 – 2025).

FOREWORD

This Easter, I was asked to do a five-minute reflection on the thief on the cross for a Maundy Thursday service at church. Rather than a general reflection on the significance of this Gospel incident (Luke 23:32-43), I decided to attempt to enter imaginatively into the world of the anonymous criminal. I suppose you could call it creative writing: the kind of thing I hadn't attempted since I was at school over 40 years ago! Looking back, I think my inspiration almost certainly came from reading a draft version of Men of Straw. John Adamson's new novel encouraged me to try and enter imaginatively into the world of a biblical character, and I ended up entering into the biblical text more profoundly as a result.

I've previously very much enjoyed reading John Adamson's contemporary "Hub trilogy" (The Informant, The Insider, and The Deceiver) – not least because of the underlying French connection in each of the novels. But Men of Straw is quite different. It's an imaginative retelling of the biblical book of Ruth, set during the period of Israel's history depicted in the book of Judges (approximately 1250-1050 BC).

As a story that deals with issues such as food scarcity, economic migration, the challenge of cultural adaptation, and the vulnerability of women in a male-dominated society, the book of Ruth is certainly relevant for contemporary readers. John's version of the story faithfully reflects the main aspects of the biblical text, but he also introduces some modern elements – teenage moodiness and shady "property management agents", for example – to lend a more contemporary flavour to the original storyline.

Filling just four pages in most Bibles, Ruth is one of the shorter Old Testament books. The main characters (Ruth, Naomi, and Boaz in particular) are beautifully delineated but, because the canvas is so small, there's little room for character development or extended dialogue. These are more the terrain of the novelist, and John Adamson enthusiastically takes up the challenge of imagining what some of the domestic joys, tensions, and tragedies might have been like between the original characters (as well as adding in one or two of his own).

Alongside his trademark humour, John's book also has a darker side with the cult of Chemosh offering some thought-provoking parallels to religious and political extremism in our contemporary world. The contrast to this is the simple but steadfast trust in the biblical God of love and faithfulness that Naomi demonstrates and shares with her family and friends.

If you've not read the book of Ruth before (or haven't read it for a while), I'd certainly recommend that you do so alongside reading Men of Straw. Read the biblical book to see what God might want to say to you through it. But also read

John Adamson's book to be encouraged to engage your imagination (and not just your reason and your emotions) when reading Scripture. I'm grateful to John for encouraging me to do that with his new novel – and I hope you will be too.

Dr Paul Cooke
June 2025

Part One

"In those days Israel had no king; everyone did as they saw fit."

(Judges 21 v 25, NIV)

"In the days when the judges ruled, there was a famine in the land. So a man from Bethlehem in Judah, together with his wife and two sons, went to live for a while in the country of Moab. The man's name was Elimelek, his wife's name was Naomi, and the names of his two sons were Mahlon and Kilion. They were Ephrathites from Bethlehem, Judah. And they went to Moab and lived there."

(Ruth 1 vv 1-2, NIV)

CHAPTER ONE

TEENAGE TROUBLES

Mahlon had been pushing his luck. Recent manifestations of awkward adolescence coupled with a growth spurt made for a contentious cocktail of teenage tensions for their vertically challenged mother. My baby boy was suddenly taller than me and I needed the help of my spouse, Elimelech.

I call him Eli for short. My name's Naomi, by the way. Anyway, back in the day, Eli was generally deemed a sound marriage prospect for me. Certainly, he was good looking as a young man, and a snappy dresser. He made all the right moves. If I'm honest, I had a few doubts back then, but I thought I could change him, and I came to believe that I loved him.

He got better, to be fair, apart from letting his dress sense slip when he was with me. Not so for business, of course. He left the mechanics of bringing up Mahlon and his brother Kilion, a couple of years his junior, to me. He had lands to manage, he said, which he described as time-consuming. To me, he was just out of the house for many an hour. If I tell you

I got used to that, you'll also understand that I didn't mind. I was there for our boys.

Don't get me wrong about Mahlon, he's a good lad. Lately, he's just made the odd wrong choice, that's all, rather like his father. But that's not for now.

Kilion is more of a mummy's boy, if you can forget any inappropriate Egyptian images which may have come into your head. From a very young age, he has always had a way of looking out for me.

So, I'm in the kitchen, gazing at the floor and pondering a course of action. Elimelech arrives. Something's going on. He's early. Has Mahlon offended him?

I think I'm in luck when he opens his mouth. "Nomes, we've got a problem. We need a chat." His troubled smile was the first thing I saw as I raised my head.

I'm not sure, so give him the benefit of a pair of shrugging shoulders. "I was going to say something similar to you. You certainly need to speak to Mahlon, Eli. He's always had a cheeky kind of humour, but nowadays he's sometimes downright rude."

He looks at me as if I'm an alien. "That isn't it. I'm talking about food." The smile slips away, leaving nothing but a few facial wrinkles.

My hopes are dashed. Mahlon hasn't caused a problem. I repeat the shoulder action and guess again. "If it's last night's dinner, Eli, it was a new recipe. I won't use it again."

Wrong again. "Last night's dinner was alright. That's not it either."

Alright? It was better than that, according to Kilion. I'm a bit irritated by now. "So, what's wrong? You're back before the usual time; it's not our son and it's not our diet. Do tell."

He sighs. "It's not you, Nomes. It's bigger than you."

I'm staring at him, hands on hips. I notice his beard is unevenly trimmed, but this isn't the time. "Most things are. Is that a culinary compliment, Eli?"

His tone revealed mild exasperation. I could always outdo him verbally, and he didn't like that. "This is no time for clever talk, or flippancy, Nomes. There's disturbing news."

He'd been talking to some relatives, it turns out. From my side, one was a second cousin of mine by the name of Boaz, a very decent chap, plus a closer family member who is admittedly hard work. Eli doesn't pay much attention to anyone's opinions but his own, so I should have noticed when he started quoting the latter. This guy doesn't relate well and, frankly, struggles with the concept of human empathy. He remains almost anonymous in family matters, so much so that Eli jokes about his inability to join in with anything at all. So, what does my husband do? He nicknames him Anon for a joke, but it mutates with use, and everyone now calls the young fellow Nonny. I ask if he was numbered among my husband's collocutors.

The discussion had not been totally collaborative. "Nonny? Yes. He was there. Didn't say much." No surprise there.

I stick with my preferred tactic, a dash of humour mixed with a de-escalation of whatever Eli was going to claim. "Eli, you used to say Nonny blows with the wind. That didn't do much for his reputation with our boys. They would wince and blame too many vegetables. Now can we talk about Mahlon's manners – or lack of same?"

We couldn't. "Nomes, you're not getting this, it's far more

serious than you think. You recall that Nonny was fascinated by keeping a weather diary as a kid?"

That's weird for a kid, even in a small town like Bethlehem. To be honest, I had forgotten, but it didn't surprise me. Eli fills me in further. "He has been keeping tabs on the weather for a couple of years now. He's a bit nerdy about it, if I'm honest."

"He was serious. About the sun, rain and wind. And you should stop Mahlon and Kilion laughing at him."

Thirteen years of married life had taken away most of my husband's sense of humour. But experience has taught me not to anger Elimelech beyond a certain point.

He pauses for a split second, so I seize my chance, admittedly with a little trepidation. I go with his laughter reference. "I can't seem to get any smiles out of Mahlon these days. You need to speak to him. He can still be witty when it suits him, but he doesn't reply in sentences these days when I ask him anything. He just uses what my father used to call non-verbal and paralinguistic utterances.

I know what's coming. "Uh? What are they?"

"Grunting to you and me." I can see I'm not getting anywhere with the issue, so I reluctantly move on. Never mind, Eli. Tell me about what Nonny briefly had to say."

I glimpse a visual acknowledgment of my strategic verbal retreat. "I'll have a word with Mahlon. Nonny? He confirmed that the climate is changing."

This blows my mind. I'm questioning if I've really heard him say what he did. I fix him with an iron look. "Do you know what that means if he's right?"

He's grimacing. "Yes. There's going to be food shortages.

Real ones. Hungry people. Famine. Got it? Shall I spell it out for you again?"

There was no need. I'm cross. He's always had the brawn and used to tell me that I was the brains of the partnership. I find myself wagging my finger assertively and give him full title. "Don't treat me like an idiot, Elimelech."

I take two steps back from him. In case. He ramps up the volume. "What's worse in life than food shortages, Naomi? Even boring Boaz gets it. Nothing! He was one of those there this morning. Listen, he is also predicting that the harvest is going to fail. Droned on for ages about it."

I've always thought of Boaz as one of my wiser kinfolks. He's a careful man of integrity and faith. He weighs up every word and speaks engagingly. I don't know him that well, but I'm told he seeks the Lord's wisdom for his life.

So, I twitch at the droning reference and retreat a couple more paces. "And you switched off when he told you about the seemingly poor outlook for the harvest, Eli? To him and to the others, I bet. Boaz could have reminded you that God is the source of all wisdom. Even our boys have been taught that it can be discerned through careful discussion with other believers. How many times do I have to tell you? Don't jump to hasty conclusions!"

He feigned a yawn before attempting to lower the temperature of the discussion. "Boaz did start waffling on, sure, but there was no time to lose. Get ahead of the game, that's what I say. We need solutions, not problems, my dear."

He has the opposite effect. He's making me feisty. I draw myself up to my full five feet. "Don't patronise me and don't underestimate him, Eli. Boaz is aware of the teachings of our nation's heritage. He will be only too well aware of the belief that God can use weather changes to show displeasure. Ignoring him will end in tears."

I couldn't believe his next assertion, delivered in a voice which was eerily both aggressive and calm. "Naomi, there are times to listen to such old fables and there are times for action. Maybe he did mention something about history and Moses, but I have a family to protect."

I'm still not for conceding but back off slightly from the confrontation. This is important. "Look, Eli, this is much bigger than you're admitting. Our nation has chosen to give men authority and powers which are not theirs to deploy. Only the Lord can judge. We're all in deep trouble. We must face up to the fact that we are his people, his chosen race, and by and large we've stopped following him."

I was right. "Boaz may have mentioned something about that. He thinks it's a national problem for sure. That's why my plan is a clever ruse."

"Don't you believe what he said, Eli?"

He ignores the question and decides to dumb down. "He knows his crops, does Boaz. Not one to go against the grain. Boaz knows. He's an expert."

I try a touch of humour to see if that has any effect. I quip "In his field, yes." He stifles a grin, so I set my face and gently re-escalate the issue. "Now think about what I told you. Boaz has been saying for some time that our nation should reconnect to the Lord. We should stick together and do as he says."

I'm winning, but he just sniffs and pulls back to a topic change, to where I began. "Let me speak to Mahlon about his manners."

He's not getting away with that ploy. I'm gritting my teeth mentally, if you follow me. He hears it straight. "Pray, Eli, pray about what's going on! And while you're doing that, pray for Mahlon too, that he doesn't ignore you as well as me. He might if he's not in the mood. Please do that soon."

He deflects the urgency. "I've got a lot on my plate, Nomes."

This irony is too much for me. "Really? When you were just on about food shortages? Get on your knees and take your plateful to the Lord. He will help you, Eli."

Our eyes meet. Is he making a concession? "If I get a minute, I'll deal with Mahlon for you."

I'm unsure but decide to pick this battle. "I bet he doesn't grunt at you, Eli. I'd like you to know how I feel."

"Maybe grunting's good from teenagers. It's how they communicate."

I anticipate his impending abdication of paternal duty. "But Kilion is starting to follow suit. He's lovely, he's caring, and quite serious. Let's not spoil that."

He's having none of it. "Come on, Nomes, it's a tough old world out there for youngsters. So much pressure, so many expectations. We were like that once."

Our culture, heritage and tradition are not ones of adolescent self-correction through experience. I try to remind him of that. "You'll regret not correcting them, Eli. It'll bring problems later. Teenagers need firm boundaries. And clear direction from their parents."

Not my most effective reply, as it turns out. He picks up the tangent and goes off on it. "As it happens, I've got the direction sorted, Nomes. The boys will more than grunt if there's no food for them. Nonny also mentioned that the neighbours had started panic buying."

I find myself retreating. "I don't like the sound of any of that, Eli, especially the direction part. Can't we at least pray? We must never take the Lord for granted."

His attempt at humour is just not funny. "Or for grunted. We need to act fast, Naomi. Time is not on our side."

I regroup after the retreat. "Listen to me, Elimelech. No good decision is rushed or made without God's wisdom. Let's seek his will. The Lord may be calling us to further service here. Don't forget that we're lucky, we've got resources."

The discussion, if that's what it was, is unilaterally drawing to a close. "And those resources, my dear Nomes, are precisely why we must act. Now."

I tell him how anxious I'm feeling. We do a lot here, and there's plenty of folk whom we support. I was brought up to do God's work and bless others with what we have. Eli doesn't see that, because he's managing his fields or hanging out, as Mahlon would put it, in the town square. Our entire lifestyle seems in jeopardy. I'm scared. So, I don't look at him as I'm leaving the room. Maybe it will be better tomorrow.

CHAPTER TWO

MAKING TRACKS

Tomorrow has arrived. He'd already gone out by the time I'd finished praying, which was longer than usual. My mind was still unsettled. Then I found his work clothes were still in the house. It was more than a couple of hours later when he returned. He was abrupt. We were leaving, he said.

I was indignant and he knew it. "And where might we be off?"

"I'll tell you in the morning. I'm going to speak to some people who can help us. It's that new property management agency in town. Their list of services extends well beyond residential lettings. They are people-focussed. They do a comprehensive moving package."

They might do that, but at what cost? He never discusses money with me, but I haven't given up asking. "Sounds awfully expensive. Do you pay them a fee?"

"Business is business, yes. Let's call it a small financial consideration. I'm taking care of it."

"Hang on, Eli, you still haven't convinced me why we have to do this."

He snapped at me unnecessarily. "Stop being obtuse, woman. If we go, whatever food there is here can be eaten by others. You, know, the ones who can't afford to get out. We're doing this to help them. The Lord will be pleased. Naomi, that's why you should be happy too."

Was he hiding something? He deflected my specific concerns about money with a generalised and vague answer. When I think back, I first felt this way soon after our wedding. Why hadn't I questioned him harder over the years? I suppose because we had all we needed. I told myself that his business must be doing well. Or was it my sixth sense that if I did push him too far one day, I'd hit a nerve and trigger a reaction that went beyond the verbal? A voice in my head told me he was controlling me, but other noises drowned it out. Giving the boys a secure and stable home was my God-given priority, so I'd kept my counsel.

Moving away from Bethlehem would affect all that. I thought we must have considerable savings, of course, but they weren't going to last for ever. I hated myself for doing so, but rightly or wrongly, I took the humble road, chose my words carefully and lowered my voice.

"You know, my dear, I am really not feeling this. You'll go and do what you think you should, but I'm going to take to my knees again and reach out to the Lord, the one who governs the destiny of Israel, because his decision is the one we should seek."

The humble road turned out to be a cul-de-sac. He brushed past me and out of it. "Must dash. People to see."

I abandoned the humility kick. "It's not the people to see, it's the places to go that bother me."

He didn't hear most of my sentence, as he was gone.

Darkness was beginning to fall when he returned. I was waiting frostily by the door, but he pre-empted my planned cold reception with a satisfied smile. "Sorted. All sorted. We're out of here. Confirmation on the morrow."

Financial ignorance notwithstanding, I wasn't buying that. "What's sorted? Out where?"

He answered each question brusquely and in turn. "Us. Where's there's food."

He saw my reaction. "Nomes, you're going to be safe. I guarantee it."

"Eli, where? Tell me. Never mind waiting till tomorrow."

His reassurance was less than comprehensive. "Away from here. I've secured the perfect spot. Would you believe it, it's not too far from our own country."

"What? Abroad? You've got to be joking."

"Those guys at the property management agency have got contacts there. They can smooth the way. They've even taken a deposit from me on a house rental."

"I bet they have. And where is this idyllic spot?"

"In Moab. Four beds, detached, garden. Upstairs terrace."

Moab? Was he in his right mind? We were at war with them five decades ago. People have long memories. Surely the Lord wouldn't do that to us? Enemy territory, and we were risking everything for a crust of bread? I downloaded my brain to this idiot of a husband.

"That's history, Naomi. Forgive and forget and all that. Anyway, there's desert views from the roof."

"The kids have grown out of sandpits. Go back to the property management agency and get your money back. Tell them we're staying in this country. I tell you; Moab won't be safe."

"We simply cannot stay here. The famine isn't just local. It's a national crisis."

"You know my heart is saying no, Elimelech. No go."

"You'll be changing your opinion when the food shortages hit, Naomi."

"I will not. If you don't want the Lord involved, think about our family and friends. They're not hitting the road for Moab. They are staying put. We'll be aliens in the place, foreigners."

He reverted to the emotional. "Nomes, how do you propose we feed our boys here? Do you want to watch your own children starve? You've got no choice."

Does he still have a better nature for me to appeal to? What was left of this man I'd married? Who would do the Lord's work in Bethlehem in my place? Panic swirled around my head before I chose flattery as my next weapon.

"You're an important man around here. You're a leader. Think again, Elimelech. Trust in the Lord. Don't ignore your wider responsibilities. What about the land you own?"

No joy. "My family can take care of the fields here. It's been agreed."

He was obviously set on project Moab, and he hadn't finished. The use of the first-person plural raised my hackles, but I kept my mouth shut as his rhetoric continued. "Responsibilities, Naomi? What about our duties as parents? Kilion and Mahlon aren't going to think much of us if we can't feed them. We've got the means to go elsewhere, where there's plenty to eat. Growing boys don't need mealy-mouthed excuses, they need tucker on the table."

Climate change isn't a respecter of international borders, and resultant food shortages weren't either. If I'd played that card, he would have countered with some nonsense about Moab's microclimate, so there was no point in my taking that line. I had no evidence to back up my case, so I followed his suit and went on the emotional approach. "Eli, I hate the feeling of running away. I'm concerned we are escaping from God's hand, abandoning all we do in his name in this place."

It was another tactical error on my part. He clicked his fingers. "I recall a rabbi recounting some years ago that Abraham moved to Egypt when there was a famine. There's proof for you."

It wasn't proof, of course. Truth mattered to me. I smiled superficially before parrying that strike. "Shame you weren't listening to what happened next. His trip to Egypt led Abraham to lie about his wife, bringing more trouble. Eli, if the Lord is sending a famine, we can't say we weren't warned. Abraham found that the Lord's purposes always prevail. You are dodging the consequences when you should be accepting them."

At last, I'd won a round, and I knew what was coming. It was a red herring. "Let's talk to the boys, Naomi. Let's see if they're up for this adventure."

"Adventure? Really? Their views? You've made your mind up. You'll pretend to listen to them, but you'll do what you plan anyway. You're selling us a done deal."

He affected conciliation. "It's about discerning the best course of action, Nomes. That's what I'm doing."

This red herring wasn't getting off the hook that easily. "There's not a lot of discerning going on here if you ask me.

You're deliberately avoiding something. Let me spell this out. God may be wanting to teach us through the famine. Your crackpot scheme is a cack-handed attempt to thwart eternal purposes and is doomed to fail. Abraham blundered by going to Egypt without God's sending. And have you prayed at all? Have we prayed together? No!"

"No need, Naomi. The Lord gave us the brains to make decisions. The Lord gave us our wits. The Lord gave us common sense. And the Lord gave all of those things to us so we would use them. We're going, Naomi, we are going. I hate feeling hungry."

I had had enough. "When will you inform the boys? Oh, sorry, weren't you going to consult them? Or did I dream that?"

"Wait till breakfast. While we can still provide one."

Chapter Three

Ships of the Desert

Neither I nor Elimelech slept well that night, but morning found my husband with renewed determination. Me? It was more an exhausted resignation mixed with regret. He told me to call the boys, which I did rather monotonously. There was no response. Mahlon and Kilion slumbered on, unaware of the impending disaster.

"Naomi, call them again now, please. Now!"

"I will, but you can handle them when they protest. Why do you treat me like this?"

"Just do it, Naomi, and watch me." He avoided eye contact as I edged away from him.

I called again. "Kilion, Mahlon, breakfast in five minutes. Your father has something he wants to tell you."

I couldn't look at him. "Done it. As you instructed."

Was there a hint of discomfort in his demeanour? I wasn't sure. "Thank you. Are they on the way?" He was hesitant.

"I heard a couple of grunts."

He smiled wanly in my direction. "That's no way to refer to them." There was a time when I would have laughed, but it was long gone. I gritted my teeth and stared at him. He caught a glimpse of my face and withdrew his attempt to reduce the tension. "So long as they get up, that's all we need."

"I'll tell them they should pray after listening to you."

"Naomi, you will not interfere. Just get the food out. I'll do the talking."

The final barb hurt, but I couldn't let it show. "Look, I couldn't sleep, Elimelech. I prayed to the Lord most of the night about all this. He told me again that we had to trust in His providence, even in suffering."

He waved my arguments away. "We do. In Moab. And heading there is precisely what we are about to do. I'll hear no more of it. We're leaving. You told me that God brought good out of what Abraham did, so whatever we do, we're covered. Now where are those lads?"

I heard their steps. There was no time to put him right, but would it have been productive? I doubted it. "They're coming now. Let them enjoy breakfast first, before you tell them."

The mood changed as they arrived, but my own cloud was dark and heavy. I felt sick when I heard his smooth opening gambit. "Morning men. Sit down."

for once was reliable. He yawned dramatically and underwhelmed his father Mahlon with a flat "Hi Dad."

His father dug a little deeper. "Tuck in, get some calories on board! We've got a big day ahead of us."

Kilion, bless him, smelt a rat. "You're very cheerful, Father. What have you done this time? What's the story?"

If I was feeling cynical, Mahlon sounded at least sceptical, albeit camouflaged within his teenage morning fatigue. "Yeah, come on Dad, spill the beans."

I'd seen it all before and sighed. "He spills food enough as it is when he's in this kind of mood."

I still couldn't look him in the eye. "You'd better tell them now, Elimelech, while they are using sentences."

Mahlon cocked his head to one side, folded his arms and looked at his dad. "Eh, wha?"

It was funny, abrupt and rude, so I waited to see Eli's reaction. He pretended he hadn't heard. "So, after we've eaten, all of you get together all your belongings. We're dropping the heavy stuff with the agents in town who will ensure it is delivered to our new address. Just make sure you keep enough for a few days. That'll be what you carry."

Mahlon's mood lifted sharply. "New address? Moving house! How exciting! Which part of town are we going to? A posh bit?"

My husband kept it vague. "Get this, Son. Location isn't the issue. We're going on a great family adventure together. We are emigrating."

Kilion sensed uncertainty and looked pleadingly at me. "Will that make us migrants, Mum? I'm not sure that's an adventure. But if you and Dad say it's okay, maybe it will be."

I was desperate to speak, but all I could do was to put my arm around him. Elimelech continued with the plural pronoun. "Have we ever let you down before? It means we get to discover a new country, Kilion. All of us together. And don't worry, there'll be no starving where we are headed!"

I squeezed my younger son tightly. Mahlon sensed something wasn't quite right with me. "Dad, we can't leave. All my friends are here. So are Kilion's. He doesn't get it, but he's too young to be uprooted, and so am I. We are Bethlehem boys through and through. And what's this about starvation? Last week the rabbi told us that Bethlehem's town name means House of Bread. We'll never run out!"

I finally managed a genuine smile, which served only to put Eli even further onto the back foot. He became stern. "Boys, get used to this. We are leaving for Moab. There's plenty of new friends waiting for you there, I'm sure. Their tables are groaning with more than a few loaves. It's where we're going, like it or not. And listen, there's a bedroom each for you."

I bit my lip over the groaning table, but Kilion spoke up. "The bedroom thing doesn't bother me. I don't mind sharing."

Mahlon saw which way the wind was blowing. He glanced at his father and moved further into my camp. Teenagers may be mercurial, but they can be more conservative than adults. He took a deep breath and took up my narrative. "Dad, the same rabbi told us what your name means too. It means 'my God is king'. So how come we're going to a place where they don't worship him? And if we do, we'll be strangers. Migrants are, sadly. And we won't make friends like we have here."

I was about to compliment him on the points he'd just made when Elimelech cut him short. "You two have been listening to that rabbi too much."

I wasn't having that. My voice came over powerfully, I thought, carrying an almighty threat. "Eli, don't speak like that!"

Did I see him bare his teeth? He was angry. "Everything's in place. I've been down to confirm times with the property management agency."

I fired off another volley, backed by my disapproving

glance. I was getting good at that. "Have you checked them out fully? Can we really trust them if they're new? Have they any track record to show you?"

"Nomes, give over on that. They're a start-up. They do move people, but they also move their belongings. Quite a lot of demand apparently. I've asked them to pick up the rest of what we have that's transportable and drop it off at the destination the day after we arrive. That's very professional. And not cheap either. I'm investing heavily in their services, and only the best will do for you and the boys. Family comes first."

Mahlon had woken up. "Those guys who arrived a few weeks back? My mates aren't over-impressed. Mum's right."

"Nonsense. That's typical when new people settle in your neighbourhood. You and your pals have never met them. I have. They're decent."

I stifled a sniff. "So how much did you pay them?"

He elected not to answer, of course. "Every business has admin costs. Listen, we're good to go. They'll see our stuff is delivered. Now it's time to get ourselves to Moab."

"And where exactly is the house?" Mahlon wanted a direct answer. Kilion raised an inquisitive eyebrow in support of his brother.

He didn't get one. "Trust me, these guys have got it all sorted. It's about fifty miles from here, that's all. They say they have got the transport booked."

"Sorry to say this in front of the boys, Elimelech, but it's not a straightforward journey that way." I wasn't really sorry. "It's a bit hilly, isn't it? And don't hills mean danger?"

"Maybe, but their men have got all that covered. Look, I

promise you, we'll take a few days down by the Dead Sea once we're established. You'll love it, all of you. The doctors are saying that sea air is good for well-being."

My eye was steely. "Never mind well-being, we'll all need to see the doctor for other reasons if you go ahead. Personally, I'd rather risk staying here, than travel through bandit territory to an alien country on the promise of a few days by the water."

That was it. Elimelech raised his hands to signify the time for talking was over. "You've got an hour, Naomi. Get the boys ready. Enough stuff for up to a week. And be prompt. There's a few of us going. My man at the agency said the price includes use of a few camels." He stormed out.

I looked at the boys. "Great. Just what we need. Travelling for days with people we've never met. This gets better and better!"

Eli's departure lifted my gloom. Kilion put both his arms around me. "Mum, perhaps the camels will get us there faster. Then you won't have much time to worry about Dad's plan."

Mahlon grinned. "Where do you guess we meet up with the camels? And the rest of the punters?"

I fell for it. "Good point. This wretched property agency must use some kind of a base."

"It'll be that desert transit site on the edge of town. All camel-convoy members join up there."

"And its name?" My question was genuine.

"The Caravan Club."

CHAPTER FOUR

HOOD

Mahlon had been right about the meeting point. Elimelech set a firm pace as we left home. Mahlon accompanied him whilst his brother took my arm after noticing a single tear trickle down my cheek. He stopped to console me until Eli gestured us to hurry. I couldn't. We only caught them up when they slowed to a halt and surveyed the scene in the distance. The site looked empty.

Kilion looked at his father and pointed. "Isn't that it? Where are all the camels?"

Mahlon's brow furrowed. "It's very quiet. Where do we meet your friends, Dad?"

None of us could avoid noticing a hint of uncertainty in Elimelech's reply. "Trust me, they'll be waiting for us. Mahlon, why don't you walk with your mum? Carry her stuff for her."

This was no act of gallantry on my husband's part, but a bid to fob me off. Mahlon took my bags, however, as we watched Eli stride off alone and at pace. The three of us adopted a gentler gait and ten minutes later, we eventually found our leader waiting at a firmly closed gate.

I could see nothing, but Kilion was first to speak. "It's like I said. There's no-one here. And not a camel in sight."

Eli affected annoyance. "Son, it was your brother's fault, his and your mother's. If you hadn't been wasting time and ambling along, we wouldn't have missed them. They must have gone without us. There's only one direction they could have taken. We'll catch them up if we walk quickly."

My exasperation boiled over. "You can if you like."

Mahlon squeezed my arm. "Don't worry, Mum. Kilion and I will stay with you. Dad can go ahead and tell them to wait for us."

Dad got the message and made to stride off. His dudgeon was high, but his younger son's plaintive tone stopped him in his tracks. "What if we don't catch them, Mum?"

I pursed my lips. "Then we've got a week's walking, Kilion. Some of it over the hills."

Their father emitted a groan as he fended off my undermining remarks. "I tell you, there's food at the end of it, everyone. Just step out bravely. We've got camels to catch."

A shout from behind made me jump. We spun round and saw a hooded man with an obvious wart on his nose. He had what Mahlon later described as the scrawniest camel he'd ever seen, which admittedly isn't that many. Eli's humour lifted immediately.

The agency hadn't let him down, he boasted to us, and here was the proof. The man whom Mahlon immediately named Hood loaded the bags on board with Eli's enthusiastic assistance and motioned me to climb on.

I refused, partly because it seemed undignified and partly because I didn't have a clue how to steer the animal. What would I do if it bolted? And which way was Moab? We needn't have worried on that score, though, as Hood was coming with us. I caught a few words of his conversation with Eli and first thought that he was speaking with an accent. Mahlon, who was nearer, said it was a similar language to our own. It all crystallised when Hood declared himself to be well acquainted with the Moabite tongue. And that's right, we can understand their language, and they can comprehend what we say.

He was full of it, Eli. The main group had gone earlier, but they'd designated this guy as our guide, how good was that? A native speaker of Moabite too. How could we have ever doubted his word, money well spent, you can work out the rest. My husband was bordering on the totally unbearable.

Mahlon was still suspicious about the suitability of Hood's dromedary. He was making the point when Eli climbed up, wobbled embarrassingly and perched awkwardly on the steed. There he was, and there he stayed, like some wannabee kingly warrior surveying the horizon. The uneven beard and iffy clothing did little for his image as he clung on. Mahlon sniggered loudly, covering it with a blow of the nose when his father risked a tumble by deigning to look down at him. And off we all went.

Hood didn't say too much but had obviously done the route before. He knew the overnight shelters, food and water stops and safest options when it got hilly. He covered all the costs en route, to Eli's approval. The camel proved reasonably resilient, to our surprise, and by the third day, I was confident enough to ride.

To be fair to Eli, he strapped all our wealth to himself

throughout the journey, never removing the belt which held the money and valuables to sell when we had resettled. We didn't know how much, but his caution gave us confidence. He was taking a giant robbery security risk and took it all on himself.

We didn't see a single bandit. Back home, the area was infamous. Hill country gives advantage to attackers, and there were legends about their exploits. There were callers one night, however, but Hood went out, said a few words, and they disappeared. Mahlon reckoned money had changed hands from the snatches of conversation he'd heard. I was just grateful we were all in one piece.

Six days in, we were within sight of Moab. Hood stopped. He told us to wait. We did as we were bid. It had been a long and monotonous journey. Even Elimelech's positivity was fading, a victim to increasing frustration and exhaustion. Me? I was okay, although the terrain was difficult when I was walking, and my pace was slow. Just as when we left home, Kilion had kept me company as Mahlon and his father led the way.

Hood, who had walked every step thus far, climbed abord the beast of burden and set off. He told Eli that he was going ahead to finalise the accommodation deal and would be back later the same evening. I sat down on a large stone. My feet were killing me. I'd walked further than ever, despite getting - if you can cope with the image – the lion's share of the camel. Those rocky paths had cut my soles into ribbons.

Eli appeared to sympathise. "Sorry, Nomes. I'm sure I'd paid for a camel each for all four of us. Probably an admin error. They'll refund me if so."

Hood returned before nightfall as promised and took us to our last refuge close to Moab. I found myself trusting Hood, who still wore the headgear, by the way. He was about to lead us into Elimelech's Promised Land. Even my feet felt better as my worry list was reduced to one item. Would the rest of our property make it to the fantastic house Eli had reserved for us? What could possibly go wrong? I voiced my concern.

Mahlon was straight in. "Dad, they'd better find us. Or else. I've got clothes in those bags. And my new fragrances."

Kilion's expression turned to puzzlement. "What?"

His brother's voice was confident. "Kil, you have to smell nice if you want to make friends."

"That's not true. If you've chosen it, it probably smells worse than you do normally."

"Careful, you might get a slap, little bro."

Kilion wasn't put off. "My friends don't use perfume."

Mahlon peered at him. "Deodorant, Kil. Fragrances. You're forgetting. We're talking new friends. The old ones are still in Bethlehem."

Kilion countered swiftly. "Weren't you wanting to stay with them?"

Mahlon's cheeks reddened briefly. "It is what it is, Kil. We deal with what we have."

Kilion found his brother's inconsistency puzzling. "And are you saying that Moab boys are different?"

Mahlon was ready to deliver the coup de grace. "Ah. I'm talking about girls, Kilion. Girls."

His brother's expression changed to one of mock horror. "Girls? Ugh!"

Mahlon smiled knowingly. "You'll change your mind one day, little bro. Trust me."

Elimelech held up a hand to end their banter. I grinned secretly at the pair of them, but to be honest, my mind was still wandering to what the next morning would bring.

Chapter Five

The Promised Land

Hood was as good as his word. We left at first light and entered Moab. An hour later, a town hove into view. We stopped for a moment to allow Elimelech to take my place on the camel. He muttered something to Hood, who gave him a thumbs up. A short conversation followed, just out of earshot.

The dialogue concluded, my husband steadied himself by grabbing the animal's most obvious back protrusion and re-assumed the wobbly conquering hero pose. Mahlon whispered to me that his father had taken the hump, and I giggled.

He was a man on top of his game. "Now then boys, I like the look of this town. Our guide has just told me that our house is near the centre. He saw it yesterday. When we get there, there's to be no unseemly squabbling. First impressions count. Our new neighbours will be looking. Our guide and I will need a couple of hours when we hit town. You three are to stay in the square where we drop you. Kilion, you are to find your mum some water."

It happened as he said. Mahlon and I sat to wait, whilst Kilion fulfilled his father's task. I reflected on the morning's events, questioning whether Eli's disdain for my opinions had developed into an over developed sense of entitlement. He knew my feet were bad, but he made me walk the last stretch whilst he rode. I decided now was not the time to have it out with the man. The spectacle had given us a good laugh, and maybe he thought he would impress the neighbours, to depict him as a man of some status. I just wished he hadn't looked so ridiculous, and I decided to move on.

When he returned, he was alone. Hood and the camel were gone. He found me bathing my feet in the water whilst Kilion and Mahlon looked terminally bored.

"What's up with you two?" Their father affected surprise.

There was no point in beating about the bush. "They're bored."

"Not for much longer. I have found the house. Turns out it's around the corner from here."

Kilion helped me to my feet. Eli indicated the direction and took the lead. Moments later, we were approaching our new and much vaunted residence. Elimelech's grin was extensive as he ushered us through the main entrance. "Come on in! Home sweet home!"

I threw a glance into the first room and was met by an overpowering stink. Were those bloodstains I could see by the door? It was grim. I made my feelings known.

Elimelech waved my comment away. "It's handy for the marketplace. Not far to the town centre. There are three water sources nearby too."

Mahlon couldn't resist that one. "Well, well, well!"

I chuckled but managed to hold a serious face as the house tour evolved. "Eli, it's filthy, and too small. I'm struggling to see the four of us in here even if we scrub the place. Remind me, when does all our stuff arrive?"

Elimelech shrugged and ignored the issue. He told me we had to manage. I wasn't up for that. "Two bedrooms. You said four. And it's grim. The neighbourhood looks dodgy too."

He looked at me in the most patronising manner he could summon up. "Don't judge a book by its cover, Nomes. And the new neighbours? They were waving to us as we walked past their houses."

Mahlon intervened. "I would describe their hand movements differently, dad. Gesturing is closer to the truth."

I inhaled sharply on hearing this. "Eli, tell me that you haven't paid anything out beyond a deposit on this dump yet?"

Would he have told us? Probably not. It wasn't just the camel who had taken him for a ride. "Nomes, I got a great deal. Big discount and only six months up front. Mind you, the cost of living here is a lot higher than at home. This house is all they had available."

"What happened to the super villa property with all mod cons that you reserved back home?

"It seems there was a mix-up, apparently. Not the fault of these guys here. We were lucky to get this one, and that was thanks to our guide. The last tenants left unexpectedly, yesterday."

I smelt a rat. "And Hood sorted that out yesterday after he'd left us on our own for the day. I can't say I'm surprised. And a bit too convenient by my reckoning."

"God provides, Naomi. That's what you always tell me. I believe that Hood, as you call him, was used for God's purpose. Didn't you tell me that's how the Lord operated in our history?

He had me there. "I feel very uneasy, Eli. Nothing's right, nothing. How and when will we get our belongings delivered, if ever?"

He attempted to placate me. "Leave the worrying to me, my dear Nomes. When Hood took me to greet his colleagues here earlier, they were expecting me. The whole process is in hand."

My brow furrowed. I was being patronised even more. "Did I hear you right? Hood must have gone there yesterday. Of course they were expecting you. With what you will have forked out, I should think the red carpet would have been more appropriate!"

Elimelech's grip on financial secrecy remained tighter than ever, but I spotted that he shuffled to hide his embarrassment. "Well yes, it even felt like God opened that door."

I hadn't finished my piece. "God? He doesn't charge for his services. If you've made a mistake, for his sake, tell us.

He looked at the floor. "I have not. These guys here were so sympathetic, and amazed when I told them we'd walked here. They were so kind. That's why they gave me the discount. Kindness personified."

I had a further question. I needed details. "Okay, I'll take that if you tell me at what price did their kindness come?"

No deal. "Never mind that, Nomes. You wouldn't understand. These folks are linked to religious people here. I thought you might like that."

"Chemosh followers, by any chance? The Moab god? Or should I call him by what he is, an evil spirit?

He couldn't look me in the eye. "There was a statue in the background there, yes. But maybe it brought us good luck."

"Don't even think like that, Elimelech. We should have nothing to do with this. Nothing whatsoever. Let's cut our losses, however big they are."

It seems this is all my fault. Elimelech went on the offensive. "You've never been great at accepting gifts like this discount, have you? Giving them is no problem to you, but you don't take them easily."

"No, that's true. Unlike you, I need to be sure about the giver's motives."

"I'm telling you, my dear, this is straight from the Lord."

"We'll see. But I'm not at peace with all this, Eli, it's not good."

Elimelech's response was to abruptly change the topic. "Where are the boys? They were here a minute ago."

"Probably slipped out to explore the neighbourhood. I'll call them in. They'll be sharing the second bedroom. I'm not looking forward to this, but can we decide which will be ours?"

"Yes, I'll come up now. Like you said, you'll need to flick a duster round both, I guess. We'll need the bigger room."

"A duster? Eli, they are grimy. Those old beds look rotten. But the boys should have the larger space. You did promise them a room each, remember."

Elimelech pursed his lips before shaking his head. "No way did I promise them. The bigger room is ours. My offer to the boys was made before we missed the departure time for the camels. If you hadn't been so slow, we'd have got the bigger house."

I couldn't help myself. "Where's your family integrity, man? You'll make us seem no better than your property management pals."

Eli's hackles rose. "I'll pretend I didn't hear that. This room's got a lovely statue in the wall cavity. Local character, Naomi. The one in the agency here was like it."

I restrained myself. "Local alright. It has an inscription. Fear Chemosh."

Elimelech looked at her. "Is that really a problem? A bit of native colour over the beds?"

"A problem? It most certainly is."

"Look, Nomes, Chemosh is obviously big around here. Knowing that will help us settle in, you know, understand the community. Good for the boys too. We'll leave the statue where it is."

"What? You'll be telling me this one will bring us good fortune too. I can't believe I'm hearing this."

"Naomi, we're renting. It's not our property. You'll be quite happy if it brings more luck, especially for Mahlon and Kilion".

My voice rose an octave to show my incredulity. "Are you really saying that this mess was made by the Lord? So now you want to rely on an evil spirit to sort it out. Unbelievable."

He retained a semblance of calm, despite seething within. "I mean they'll need a bit of luck meeting new friends. Being aware of what they think their god can do can only help matters. Logical."

I attempted sarcasm. "You'll be wanting them to join the local branch of Chemosh Youth next."

It backfired. "What harm can it do, Nomes?"

Chapter Six

The Smell of Success

That evening, I overheard the two boys talking. I moved to where I could see them, but out of their sight. And what I heard brought me a limited measure of relief.

Kilion pushed his brother playfully. "Sharing a room again, mate. And not much of a view."

Mahlon smirked. "You said it wouldn't bother you. But get this, little bro. I may have made a new friend while we were out."

Kilion raised an eyebrow. "That was quick. What's his name?"

Mahlon drew himself up to his full height. "We're not talking a 'his', Kil, we're talking a 'her'."

"A girl? Really? I'm still not excited by that news."

"Time you grew up. She may have a nice younger sister, or a suitable friend."

Kilion shook his head vigorously. "I don't think so. Anyway, how did you meet her? I thought I'd been with you all day since we arrived in this dump."

"She was sitting on the steps of a house just down the road.

Kilion, I'll teach you something. It was the way she looked at me. Us men, we can just tell."

"Really? Can we? And that's without your deodorants. Mind you, she was a few yards away. That probably helped. She won't be impressed by our residence though, no chance."

Mahlon gestured vaguely up the road. "Maybe we'll get the bags through tomorrow, smellies and all."

Tomorrow dawned. I'd gone out early to find some breakfast for the family. Eli had been right about the cost of living, but I had no choice but to pay. When I got back, Elimelech was trying desperately to raise morale after a night which brought little comfort as well as sleep.

"Food, you see! Breakfast on the table! I told you we'd eat well here."

It wasn't fine dining, so I didn't respond. It was Mahlon who took the baton, and he worried me. I blamed myself for raising my hopes last night. He was serious. "Maybe it was that little statue we have in our bedroom. Perhaps it might be something of a lucky charm. We need to find more about it, Kil, if we are going to get to know a few girls. We can tag along when they go to worship this Chemosh and ask a few questions."

I bit my lip. Now was not the time to intervene, but I listened out keenly and silently blessed my younger son as he spoke. "I don't like his name. He sounds horrid to me."

I confined myself to a nod. "Me too."

Any further contribution was thwarted. Eli looked outside the door. "The bags are here! They found us!"

Scant consolation, it seemed, but I smiled. "Before anyone says anything else stupid about that statue, could someone please pass me that new dress your father got me in Bethlehem last month? I haven't had a proper change of clothes for weeks."

"Careful, Mum. It might be better left in the bag, given the state of this place."

Eli stroked the longer side of his beard. "You can start on the house after breakfast, Naomi. A day will make such a difference."

I'd been expecting that, but I needed to know about my clothing. "Is it there, Mahlon?"

He scanned the luggage. "The white one? I can't see it here. Are you sure you packed it?"

"Packed my new dress? For certain. I was going to wear it for my so-called wellbeing days by the Dead Sea. The treat your father promised me."

Elimelech checked. "That dress is not here. You must have forgotten it. Perhaps it wasn't meant to happen."

I stared him full in the face. "Neither was the Dead Sea trip, if I'm honest. It never was."

Mahlon put the last bag down. "Actually, there's not a lot of clothing here at all. Yours, mine or anyone else's. Looks like all the newer stuff has gone."

I could control myself no longer. "The luggage has been ransacked. We've been robbed. Where was that wretched statue when you needed it? It's nonsense, like the rest of this disastrous escapade."

Mahlon's face fell. "Oh no! Are my fragrances there? Have they gone too?"

Kilion's attempt to lighten the mood was ill-judged. "Well, that's a stroke of luck! Thank you, Chemosh! Your plans are right up the creek, Mahl. You'll have to rely on your, erm, natural aromas."

Mahlon escalated the row. "What are you saying, Kil? Are you saying I stink?"

Elimelech gestured to me to restore a semblance of calm. Always me. My fault. He had far more important executive man tasks to do. However, I put this one firmly back in his court. "Boys, enough. Your father will sort this mess out."

He had to take the bait. "I'm sure it's a simple mistake. They'll be down with the property management agent. Valuables get special arrangements, they told me. Either way, I'll go and report the oversight."

I pointed to the door. "And demand your money back."

Two hours later, Elimelech pushed the door. "I'm back. Sorry it's been a while. They are all such nice people. They took me for a drink. Very pleasant."

I saw nothing in his hands to reassure us, so I smirked. "Where are our clothes, Eli? Where's our money?"

He ignored the latter question. "The luggage caravan was attacked by bandits when they were still travelling in our country, Nomes. And they stole anything worth selling. Imagine that. People will stop at nothing. Probably our own people too. What a good job it was that we came here."

"I'll take that as meaning you have brought nothing back with you. No clothes, no money."

"Well, there's progress on the financial front. It seems that the guys here were linked to the Bethlehem agency. They said they'd take it up with them."

I wore the look of one who'd heard it all before. "And how much did they charge for asking on your behalf?"

Elimelech feigned astonishment. "Nothing, Nomes, nothing. I'm not stupid. I did give them a small tip, though."

I snarled. "I'd have given them a tip. To get out of town before I go and give them a piece of my mind. What are you playing at, Eli?"

Mahlon had been waiting his moment. "Dad, any ideas about my deodorant?"

Kilion had heard enough. He weighed in with barbed sarcasm. "Oh yeah, the robbers would have prized that. No chance, Mahl. They'd keep it in case they met any nice local girls. No brainer."

Mahlon wisely decided to ignore the jibe. "Dad, did you get it?"

Elimelech waved a hand in the air. "Sorry Mahlon, no. That must have gone too. I'll get it replaced for you."

Kilion grinned. "Can I have some? My brother says I'll be needing some soon. It's only fair that if he gets some, so should I. We don't want it going missing twice, do we?"

The family unity which Elimelech's mouth proclaimed that he valued so much was in danger of collapse, so I called it out. "We're being rather selfish, aren't we? How do we move on? Next thing, your father will be telling us that there's nothing left of our money. Even if there's food in Moab, we still need the wear-with-all to buy it."

My husband was prepared for this one. "There's enough money for all our needs for now. You can count on me for that. But medium term, we need a provisional plan, and I just happen to have one. He pointed at his two sons. "Jobs, that's how. Three of them. This family may need to rally round and create some income."

Mahlon let out a low whistle. "I think I'd rather go home, Father, if you don't mind. Bethlehem."

Kilion nodded before attempting another wind-up. "What about this girlfriend of yours, big bro? Is she coming with us?"

For the first time, incredulity spread across both our features, but mine was feigned. I left it to Elimelech to verbalise his thoughts. "What's this? Girlfriend? You're a fast worker."

Unfortunately, he misconstrued my expression as support. "Your mother and I know that we can't move back. Her job will be to keep the house and look after us. Mahlon. Kilion, you two and I need to find work. Bethlehem isn't an option. Let's all stick together."

Mahlon's shrug was overshadowed by Kilion's response. He smiled at me before moving on. "I'll buy you a dress, Mum, with my first pay packet. Mahlon, we can improve the way you smell, bro, once we've got jobs."

Chapter Seven

Secrets

The house improved. Its cleaner status perhaps emboldened Mahlon's attempts to educate his sibling further. As they strode out next day, he paused on the path. From the other side of the door, I heard him speak. "Watch and learn, Kil. Watch and learn."

Kilion was unimpressed. "Watch what?"

"I'm going to show you how to get a girl."

"Yeah? You've no deodorant. That's a problem, if I understand you right."

Mahlon stroked an imaginary beard on his chin as he had seen his father do with the real thing. "To me, there's no such thing as problems, Kil. Just opportunities."

Kilion remained low-key. "And just how does that work?"

"We'll use a cunning strategy, little bro, that's how. I'm going to ask her which deodorant she recommends. Get her advice. Then her name."

"I've got to see this, Mahl. I'll come with you."

"You won't. First lesson. Never let anyone cramp your style. Just watch from the gate."

Kilion's demeanour moved to the mischievous. "I certainly will. I'll stay with Mum whilst you go down there."

Mahlon held up his right hand to stop his sibling. "No way. Brotherly secrets, that's what we'll have. We're going to have a few of those if we're intending to make a go of living here. Especially if we have to work for a living. Find a reason to make sure Mum stays in the house, then come back out and watch me."

Kilion wasn't convinced. "Secrets? You mean keep stuff from Mum and Dad?"

"That's precisely what I mean. It's a maturity thing, Kil. We are only doing it to stop them worrying about us. Especially Mum. I'm off."

I'd heard every word, of course, and smiled to myself. Kilion came back and led me gently into the kitchen. He didn't do his brother's bidding, though. I was pleased he chose to stay with me. Ten minutes later, we heard a shout before Mahlon was back, somewhat breathless.

As he hurried through the entrance, I retreated strategically upstairs and was pleased to hear Kilion taking the initiative to head off his brother's questions.

"That didn't take too long, big bro. I couldn't hear your conversation from here, but I'm guessing you did most of the talking. Were you successful in the odourless engagement?"

"You wouldn't know this, Kilion, but the first step is always the hardest."

"Ah, went wrong, did it?"

"No, not entirely. You are reckoning without my charm. She told me a name."

"Hers, or the one for the deodorant?"

"I thought it was the latter, Kil. Her dad appeared and he shouted the same thing."

"What happened next? Is that when you ran back here?"

"Yes. He made a few gestures in my direction and yelled at me. I decided I'd achieved enough for a first meeting, and jogged home."

"Jogged? You legged it! What did he call out?"

"Probably the name of the fragrance. I wasn't sure, but in our language, it sounded like 'camel dung'. Made me laugh. I must have misheard."

"If you didn't, I don't think that'll be a best seller, big bro. Are you sure he was referring to deodorant? They won't sell many bottles of that one if you're right."

I was up early the next day and managed to acquire some bread, but there wasn't much choice at the market. Moab was no gourmet's paradise.

Mahlon was unfazed when he came down. He had not slept well and motioned to his brother to join him outside. If this was an attempt at secrecy, it failed.

I heard Kilion first. "What's on your mind, Mahl?" His tone suggested mild concern.

"It's the camel dung, Kil."

"You're not telling me she dropped a sample bottle off late last night, Mahl? You haven't splashed it on? I can't smell anything."

"No, Kilion. I've been thinking it through. You were right. She meant me. It was me that she called 'camel dung'."

"Are you sure she was so polite? Why would she do that, bro?"

"Possibly because I'm a foreigner. I'm different."

"That's all of us in the same boat, Mahl. Or on the same dromedary. You, me and the parentals."

"True. But on the bright side, at least she's noticed me." He paused for dramatic effect and resumed his previous role as a man of the world. "Women are like that, Kilion."

I was proud of his brother's response. "Like what, oh wise one?"

"They don't say what they mean."

"Mum does. She'd tell you to give them a wide berth in future."

Mahlon clasped his hands together. "Hmm. I hear you, little bro, but keep the faith in me. Getting girls is a life skill."

"If you say so. Mahlon, I'm not feeling good about all this."

"Kil, that's because you don't know what to do. I've told you, be my apprentice. I'll train you!"

"I'll need a bit of convincing after what's just happened, Mahlon. Dung isn't a great place to start!"

"That's just where you are wrong. It's all part of the game, little bro! Girls do that when they really like you."

"I wouldn't like to see what they do when they hate you. Especially when you're foreign. Anyway, I'm sure Mum was never like that."

They both laughed and came inside.

Chapter Eight

An Unanswered Prayer

The next day, unusually, Elimelech was last to get up.

"Nomes, where are the boys? I've called them but there's no reply."

I pointed. "Outside. They're staring at the house."

"Why? Is there something wrong? I'll go and see the property management agents if so."

I glanced through the window. "The boys are coming in now. Ask them."

Mahlon arrived, a little breathless. "Mum, have you got a cloth?"

Kilion was two paces behind. "Mum, make that two."

Elimelech smiled knowingly. "Good lads! Keen to help! Now what exactly is the problem?"

Mahlon sniffed. "Someone's done a drawing on the wall of the house."

His father raised an eyebrow. "Oh? What of?"

Mahlon was straight to the point. "Dung, Father. Camel dung."

I looked concerned. "Why would they do that, Eli?"

Kilion chirped up first. Eli wasn't for responding. "Mahlon got called it yesterday by the people down the road. Or it might be a local perfume brand."

I turned to my elder boy. "Why would they do that, Mahlon?"

Kilion intervened again to try to placate me. "Don't worry, Mum, it's something and nothing. Mahlon and I will get it cleaned off."

I smiled briefly before addressing my husband. "I don't like it, Eli. This sort of thing makes me very nervous."

He tried where Kilion had failed. "I'm sure it will be fine, Nomes. Probably just kids having fun. I'll report it to the property management agency this morning. They'll have words, I'm sure."

I wasn't having it. "Mahlon, I'm sorry. You shouldn't have to cope with insults."

Mahlon's tone was less than convincing. "I'm fine, Mum."

Elimelech raised a hand. "Got it! They maybe think we are to do with the previous residents. The ones who left in a hurry. We did arrive very soon after their departure. They've mixed us up. It'll stop when they realise what kind of people we are."

I shrugged. "Well, you can ask your new friends at the agency about them too. We haven't heard the end of this, I fear."

Later that day, Mahlon spotted his father approaching the house and ran down to meet him. "It all cleaned off ok, Dad. Mum's quite pleased."

I appeared more quickly than either of them had bargained for. I motioned to them to come into the house. They obeyed, then Elimelech began his prepared speech. "I had a good chat with the agents. The matter can now be considered closed."

That was less than helpful in my book, so I dived in. "What do you mean, closed? You expect attitudes to us, refugees from a country they all hate, to change just like that? All thanks to your Chemosh-sponsored agency?"

Kilion backed me up. "Mum's right, Dad. And Mahlon got shouted at again when we were outside just now. Same thing. And they were pointing at me and laughing."

His brother wagged a finger. "I won't let that happen again little bro. Neither to me nor to you."

Elimelech was floundering. "Right. The agent promised to send someone round, Naomi. And you two, listen to me. They'll deal with it, not us."

I was not for letting go. "And how much did that cost you?"

Elimelech stared at the floor. "They have expenses, you know. I just covered those for them. They also offered to protect the house for us. I refused. It was too expensive."

I'm afraid I remained unimpressed. Did I believe him? I could only find a few words. "Eli, I'll speak to you later about that."

Mahlon's attempt at a compromise was pure bravado, I shook my head, although I appreciated the sentiment. "Look, Mum, me and my bro can protect this house for you."

From the corner of my eye, I saw Elimelech nod in their direction.

A full week went by, and life was grinding me down. I felt frustration, of course, but my sense of fear was exacerbated by the daily experience of finding graffiti on our home. Mahlon and Kilion had given up on cleaning it off, but the worst thing was the name-calling. We never saw the aggressors' faces, of course. My husband's story about it being a problem of the previous occupants was wearing thin. I told him of my fears.

He was immediately dismissive. "We men can take it. They won't touch you, Naomi."

"They already have mentally. Those hidden mouths calling their filthy insults. I'm scared. Did you ever find out why did the last people vacate this property?"

"I did. They were refugees like us. It seems to me that they ran out of cash."

"So did they go home?"

"I guess so. The agents told me that one minute they were there, the next minute they were gone. Bit of a midnight flit."

"Eli, be honest with me. Did these agents confirm it was a money issue?"

He looked away. "They asked me if I wanted their security staff to watch over the place for us. I declined politely, but it's something we might need to consider."

My demeanour changed. "Elimelech, stop being evasive. I'm asking about whoever was here before us. Was it financial?"

"Not exactly." He hesitated. "But they did say that they were in debt."

"And you think that's why they went? Or was it more sinister? There were bloodstains, remember."

"Animals, probably. Yes, they were up to their ears in what they owed, the only way out was to flee. It's been done before."

"It has. But are you being deliberately stubborn here, Eli? Did your so-called agency friends bleed them dry and then step up the threats till the poor people had no choice but to run for their lives? Eli, can we just go home? I don't want to stay here. We're next on the hit list, I tell you."

"Nomes, calm down. You're getting hysterical. The other family probably didn't plan well and didn't have the resources we have. Being accepted in a new community takes time and investment."

I stopped him with a raised hand. "Look. You are a fool if you carry on like this. I prayed to the Lord when we arrived in this dump. I asked him to show me how this was his plan, and how we were to take it forward together. He has not answered my prayer."

Elimelech feigned sincerity. "The Lord loves his people. He wouldn't want us to starve in Bethlehem, would he? No way. He's answering your prayer, my dear, but you aren't listening. Doesn't our tradition tell you that you are to honour your husband and remain at his side, and comply with his decisions? The Lord wants you to do what's best for the family, and I know what that is."

I stared at the floor. "Then you're a bigger fool that I thought. You are going to drag us all down. I'm angry and frustrated, Eli, deeply. You're pushing me into a well I won't be able to climb out of, and you don't seem to care."

Elimelech affected shallow concern. "I understand, my dear. It's only natural that you feel like this. Let's give the situation some thought. Time to reflect, to look back, to see the lessons we can learn, and then plan a way forward together, you know, as a family. There, that's what we'll do."

I decided that the best response was silence. Then I sat down in a corner to pray quietly. Elimelech went out, and the rest of the day passed without external disturbance. That night, however, I didn't sleep. The next morning, though, Elimelech unexpectedly called the family together. Had he changed his mind? I was soon to find out.

Chapter Nine

Fighting Talk

Dawn, well, dawned. An hour later, we were round the table. He had finally fixed his facial hair.

Eli took charge. "Your mother and I have been talking. We think it's time to take stock on our adventure together so far."

Mahlon grunted. "Why?"

"Son, there's been a few teething difficulties, let's be honest."

I intervened. "Teething difficulties? Is that what they are? Abuse, graffiti, large sums of money paid out, and more to come for security."

Elimelech was caught unawares. "Erm, yes, your Mum's right, but listen, boys, she didn't sleep much last night. She's understandably tired this morning."

Kilion threw his mum a quick glance. "You okay, Mum?"

Before she could reply, Elimelech had recovered his poise and moved on. "Mahlon, Kilion, I have a plan."

I was not to be left out nor deflected. "So do I, after all the problems we've had. It's called 'going home'."

Elimelech managed a weak smile. "We're not going to be defeated by a few verbals and a bit of writing, are we?"

I stood up. "Those are just the symptoms. What we're dealing with here is side-stepping the Lord's plan, not trusting him to provide, and relying on ourselves and not him."

Elimelech looked the two boys in the eye. "Hear me out. I have a plan. Naomi, can you get the breakfast food out? There are three hungry men around this table."

Ten minutes dragged by. The three ate well, but I couldn't eat. I remained at a distance and looked on. Eventually, Elimelech spoke. "Ok everyone. Your mum has a point. No-one can deny that we've all suffered in the last few weeks. We need to talk strategy."

Kilion turned round and smiled at me. "Do you mean going home, Dad? I'm think I'm up for that. I don't like it here either. Mum's right."

Mahlon dissented strongly. "She's not! I say we stay and fight."

I couldn't suppress a sigh and returned to the table. "Mahlon, no-one's doing that. Let's all listen to your father and hear him out."

His father nodded. "Ok. Let's all relax for a few minutes and try to draw back from what we face every day. Kilion, how can we help you to settle here?

Kilion saw my stare. "I really just want to go home."

Elimelech was irritated. "That's not what I asked you, Kilion."

Mahlon smoothed over the perceived wrinkles and became his spokesman. "My brother thinks that yes, it hasn't been easy for any of us. He just doesn't get why that's happening.

We had lots of friends back in Bethlehem and no-one disliked us. He won't want to starve by actually going back."

Anger crossed Kilion's features. "No, Mahlon, you're wrong. I want to go home. Today."

Mahlon tried again. "Kil, give it time. Listen, we're all humans, even Moabites. They just need to get used to us. We need to work out why they are treating us as if we were the dirt on their sandals."

Kilion went for it. "Stop mincing your words. It's not dirt. It's shit. I want to go home."

Elimelech was outraged at this language. "Kilion, never speak like that in front of your mother. And listen to me. There's nothing to eat at home. Going back is just not an option."

I held my arms open as he burst into tears. "Kilion, love, come and sit with me."

Elimelech pressed home his advantage before making an apparent concession. "That's agreed, then. But I do accept what Kilion says."

Kilion wiped his eyes. "So when do we leave, Dad?"

There was no concession. "Leave? I just told you, no-one's leaving. What I am saying is that I agree with you about the problem."

"Dad, Mahlon said that, not me. No-one listens to me. Only Mum."

Elimelech focussed on Mahlon. "So we have two needs. Firstly, the time has come for us to implement our plan. We've got to stop the talking and start earning some money round here. I'm not saying we are short of resources, just that we have to start pulling together, that's all."

I sniffed. "Does that include the budget for security payments to the agency, Elimelech?"

He cut me deep. "Naomi, stop sniping and stay out of this. I have more to say. We need to show these people that we are decent, working folk who they can get along with."

"And how do we do that?"

"We are going to start by working in the community for free. The rest will come. We will work as hard as anyone has ever worked."

Mahlon's brow furrowed. "We? Is that me and Kilion?"

Elimelech nodded. "You're both in this, Son. You two are going to work your socks off. Dawn till dusk, highest standards, seven days a week."

Mahlon pulled a face. "I've changed my mind. I think I want to go home."

"No way son! We're going back to my roots. Each for a different boss. We're farmers in our family. I started out doing all the menial tasks and worked my way up."

"I thought you had a lot of land, Dad."

"Son, I inherited it when my dad passed away. I didn't own it when I started out. So when the land was mine, I knew what had to be done to get the best out of it."

"And your plan is that we do the same, right?"

"Right. We make ourselves indispensable to three lucky local farmers. Then they'll take us on full time when they can't do without us. That's the three of us sorted."

Kilion had recovered his composure "What am I going to do, Dad, at my age?"

Mahlon answered for his father. "You? You'll do exactly what the farmer tells you."

Kilion's thought about pulling a face, but he had another question first. "What's Mum going to do, Dad?

"Mum's going to keep house, be available to help the other women in the town here and do a bit of straw craft work to sell."

"Has Mum ever agreed to that?" Kilion's tone bordered on the cynical.

Elimelech winced. "Sorry, Nomes, I was coming to that. I didn't get the chance to tell you first."

I was furious. "And does this master plan of yours lead us to going home to Bethlehem one day?"

"There's no point in even considering it. There's no food."

"May I suggest something even though I don't seem to get a vote?" I wasn't hopeful.

Kilion squeezed her arm. "Yeah, Dad, I don't either."

Elimelech ignored the question and addressed Kilion. "Son, your time will come. Your father has a duty to see that the best way is chosen for his family."

Mahlon bit his lip. "No-one's getting a vote here, from what I can see. But we've come a long way together, and we've got food on the table. I think we should go with it."

Elimelech grinned. "Yes, it's time to put our heads down and graft, Son."

I wasn't smiling. "May I still suggest something, Elimelech?"

He was smoother than syrup. "Forgive me, my dear. What is it?"

"We all pray for the Lord's blessing and guidance. You included, Elimelech."

"Of course, Nomes. How about this? We should give it a

full twelve months. One year from today, we call a family conference to see what to do next. We'll surely know what the Lord wants us to do by then. Now let's hear no more about the topic. I have work opportunities to find."

With that, Elimelech left the room and headed for the market square. A humdrum year was about to begin.

Chapter Ten

The Urgent or The Important?

Once it was over, I was aware that I had aged visibly over those twelve months of loneliness and rejection. Both had weighed heavily on my heart. I'd started selling some craft in the marketplace, but there was hardly a soul who had spoken to me. My prayers had moved from desperate to depressed acceptance but despite everything I somehow clung on to a strand of hope in the Lord.

Going out was not something I enjoyed, but there was one woman whom I would sit by. For the first few weeks she would smile and occasionally say a few words. She wasn't exactly a friend, but she was company for me. Then one day, she opened up.

She spoke kindly and first checked I understood Moabite, which I did. I did likewise, and with the odd hiccup, we managed. She told me to call her Sara. Her husband worked away a lot, and like me, she had a lot of time to herself. He had his own camel, she said. I knew that was a status symbol, although she didn't see it like that and was uncomplimentary about the poor creature.

Her spouse was familiar with Bethlehem from his line of work, and she knew about the famine. She was complimentary about my boys, whom she had seen around town.

I told Sara my whole story. I explained why we were here, how we were abused and threatened, how our house was targeted, and significantly, how I felt.

Over the next few months, she made a difference. She provided a listening ear. Graffiti became a problem of the past. She encouraged me with my work and treated me as an equal.

Did I tell Elimelech? No way. I was sure he would have put an end to it. His controlling of me had tightened further, and Sara was my only escape. As time went by, there was little about me that she didn't know. And I thanked the Lord for the comfort she brought me.

The evening of Elimelech's promise arrived, and I held him to his word. Mahlon and Kilion returned from work ahead of their father. I kissed them both before quietly reminding them. "My boys, the year is over. Three hundred and sixty-five days ago, we agreed to your father's plan to remain in Moab despite my misgivings."

Kilion, bless him, looked perplexed. "Agreed? I don't remember that part."

A couple of hours later as the mealtime approached, Kilion watched me. He decided on scepticism, all for my benefit. Mahlon spotted it and grinned. "Come on, bro, let's give the guy a chance. We've thrived here."

His sibling looked at him quizzically before I held up my hands, palms outstretched. I played the diplomat. "It's fine, Kilion. Negativity never improved anything. Let's agree that your father dealt with the urgent. Now it's time to talk of the important."

Mahlon let out a low whistle. "Important? Being honest, I've got it. I'm happy. I've got a job that keeps me fit, I'm working out of doors and earning a decent wage. You've looked after us well, Mum. What's not to like?"

Eli hadn't yet shown up, so I addressed my two young men. "I've been able to keep reasonable food on the table, and I'm grateful for that. Let's stay positive with your dad. But I didn't think this whole scheme was good in the first place, and I haven't changed my view."

A slightly awkward dinner followed Elimelech's return, and inevitably, the elephant in the room was exposed. I saw to that, then began by asking a question.

"Have you got many friends, Mahlon? Plenty of pals out here now?"

Mahlon decided to be realistic. "In a way, yeah. But pals? It's not quite like that, Mum. They respect me most of the time for the work I do. They aren't so keen when the boss isn't watching, and they want to slack off. I'm a bit of a nuisance then, me working flat out as Dad told me to. I'd call most of them reasonable colleagues, to be honest."

Kilion agreed. "Things are better than they were. I wish I didn't have spots, though."

I sympathised. "That's just a phase, Son. They go away eventually." I hoped I was right. "Have you got genuine friends, Kilion?"

Kilion had matured over the year. "Certainly no enemies, Mum. No-one's wishing me harm. But not like my mates back in Bethlehem. It's like there's an obstacle between us. We can ignore it but it doesn't go away. And like Mahlon, I like earning money."

Elimelech made his move. "That's all very positive. My experience is similar, except that my supervisory skills have been recognised. I cover for my boss most days."

Mahlon grinned. "So, you don't do much work, Dad?"

"I'll teach you the skills of management one day, Son."

"Tell us how we are doing financially, Elimelech." My tone was firm and calm. "We have money coming in. What about expenses?"

Elimelech scratched his nose. "Nomes, we're keeping our heads above water and a bit more. We're doing ok. And your craft sales have gone up. At this rate, you'll be taking on staff soon."

My sales up? I hadn't noticed. I took a sip of water. "Staff? Haha."

My next question was a trap. "I hope we don't pay those property management agency people anymore. They've stopped calling at the house now."

He fell for it. He'd told us ages ago that he'd stopped. It was a lie.

A mental picture of Sara flitted into my mind as he launched into his speech. "Yes, and I'll tell you why, Naomi. Once the community here saw what kind of people we were, we didn't need further protection. I was right to do it at the time, and right to stop it as soon as possible."

"It's true that the anti-social stuff has stopped. The graffiti, the insults, everything. I am grateful for that, but we shouldn't over-estimate this. Rather like banging your head on a brick wall, it's nice now it has stopped."

It occurred to me that this development might have a link to Sara. I hoped it did.

Elimelech went onto the offensive. "Things are still pretty desperate back home. I heard that some people had starved to death."

Really? That sounded grim. Sara's husband still hadn't mentioned that to her. He said that malnutrition was causing problems, but nothing more. Was it true? I thought not, but deep down, I realised that I didn't know.

Mahlon bought into the tragic tale and was visibly moved. "Dad was right. We're best here."

His father nodded his agreement. "What I haven't told you is that I've been offered a four-year contract with a new project for my boss. More money, and a great challenge."

Kilion shrugged. "Mum, I get a feeling we're staying here."

Before I could speak my mind, my husband spoke his. "We are, my boy, we are. There's life and hope for us in Moab. Your challenge is to turn your acquaintances and colleagues into friends – all of you. And that includes your mum."

As usual, he had gone too far, and didn't stop there. I felt my face turn pale as Mahlon responded to his father's comments. "We'll need to get into the local culture if we do that. Maybe pretend we have a genuine interest in their god. He's called Chemosh. They all seem to think he's okay, if you keep him sweet."

He'd put it on a plate for his dad. Elimelech's smile was broad. "That's what's missing in your relationships, both of you boys. Why not? Play along with the idea. See where it gets you!"

My fury boiled over. "We can't do that. Our God is the

Lord. There is but one God. Chemosh is either a figment of the imagination, or worse. There is no good to be found there. It's all empty."

Elimelech tried to placate me. "Come on Nomes, what harm can it do? You're taking it all too seriously. We're only going to pretend. Beliefs won't change!"

Mahlon liked what he heard. "Then we can meet some proper girls, Mum. Get us off your hands!"

Kilion took me by the hand. Proper girls were not a prospect I was relishing.

Chapter Eleven

Blessing

Those four years weren't great for me. Sara's continuing friendship was tiring at times. She had so many questions for me, more than before. I wanted to reciprocate, to show interest in her family, but she always reverted to mine.

I did find out one thing which would have scared Kilion. Sara's husband had some kind of facial blemish which embarrassed him so much that he covered his face whenever he could. I hoped Kilion's spots would heal. This chap had one that hadn't, poor man.

I blessed the Lord again and again for sending Sara, despite the conversation being predominantly one way. She grew progressively, and maybe a tad obsessively, to know Bethlehem and its residents almost like a native, and that didn't help me because I still wanted to go back.

Neither did it help one evening when Mahlon looked up from the table. "Mum, do you remember when we were little?"

I inclined my head towards him. Our time in Moab had brought little for me to smile about, but my son's go-to question about happier days briefly cheered me. "Little? You were great kids. Where did it all go wrong?"

I was joking, but my expression had changed, and he was unsure, so he played safe. "Nothing went wrong, Mum. You've always been great."

"What's brought this on, Son?"

"It's just that you and Dad used to tell us stories about our family back home. Kilion and I were talking last night, and we want you to do that again."

"I remember those times. I'm not sure I could do that again. It's like that part of my life has ended. I remember the bones of events, but not the emotions. I've lost those. They've been taken away."

Mahlon hugged me. "Mum, Dad has a few days left on his work contract, doesn't he? Aren't we having that family conference? Maybe we could all decide to take a break."

I had to be realistic. "We didn't get a say in any decision last time, Mahlon. Your father won't want to go home. The famine is still in our land."

"To be honest, Mum, things are good here. I don't want to go home."

"But I do, Son. I'll remind you of why when we all get together."

As evening fell a few days later. Elimelech had clearly had a good day. He beamed at me as he came in. "That looks a great dinner, Nomes. We really eat well here."

That old agenda was back. I retorted "We do. Like we did in Bethlehem."

"Not the going home speech again? I've promised the boys we'll talk after the meal. I hope we're not going to fall out."

"Me too. If you listen to what I'm saying, and we won't."

"You mean about going back? I always listen. It's about time we took stock of what we've achieved here."

"Eli, have you prayed sincerely about all this? I certainly have."

He ignored my question. "Positives, Nomes, please. Not old ground. Successes. Like food on the table. Would you say that we are over the worst of the teenage behaviour thing? That's certainly a bonus."

"I suppose so. But that doesn't depend on where we live, Eli."

"And how has our wisdom increased because of that?"

"Wisdom comes from knowing the Lord, Eli, not from successfully managing teenage development towards manhood."

"There's the knowledge which comes with age, Nomes. It makes us better people. We learn and we move on. Don't do yourself down."

I decided again to keep Sara from him. "Eli, that's not true. When you get older, you develop new faults. Anyway, there's many a day when I couldn't get much lower. If it wasn't for the boys, I'd have no hope that this nightmare might ever end."

"The Lord hasn't answered your prayers, Naomi, because we're doing His work for him. And the boys are aware of their faults. The other day, Mahlon asked me what the definition was of an idiot."

"Did he just stare at you, by any chance?"

The irony was lost. "He did, actually, now you mention it. In admiration. He wanted my wisdom, so I told him."

"And what did you say? I can't wait to hear this one!"

"I defined it as a person who took ages to explain something in odd ways. At the end of it, I told him that the person he was talking to was even more confused than before. I asked him if he understood."

"Did he?"

"He just said 'no'. I guess that's teenagers today for you."

"Eli, are you sure that was what Mahlon was thinking?"

"You think I'm stupid, don't you? You're so wrapped up in yourself these days. You've got little to say to anyone. I send Kilion to cheer you up but even he comes back depressed. For heaven's sake, Naomi, snap out of it. I'll tell you what, I'm going to drive this family project forward until we prosper as much as we did in Bethlehem, then more. One day, you'll see, and you'll be proud of me. I'll call the boys now. We'll eat, then we'll talk."

"Right. That was your strategy last time. Everyone is more amenable when they are fed. Today, Elimelech, dinner will come after you've said your piece, not before. Or you can serve it yourself."

"Nomes, stay calm. I can see you are upset. Don't you think I see your pain on a daily basis? Don't you think I care? Of course I do."

"Then get me out of this hole."

"You're simply not yourself. I have to see the bigger picture, plan ahead, see the future and work towards achieving it. I have your best interests at heart. The boys are coming now. Brave face, please."

They appeared. Eli's dander was up, which annoyed me. He kicked things off. "Mahlon, take a seat. It's five years to the day since we arrived here. Let's take a few minutes to talk through where we are up to. Where's Kilion? I thought he was with you."

"He's gone back upstairs, Dad."

"What's he doing this time?"

"He's still trying to get rid of those spots on his cheeks."

I heard this, thought of Sara's husband and hoped Kilion didn't do anything to make them permanent.

Eli was getting tough. "I've been meaning to speak to you about this, Mahlon. You shouldn't have called him that name, Mahlon. He's at a very sensitive age.

"I only said it once. And what's wrong with 'crater face'? It was a joke."

"Son, he's very proud of his appearance. You should respect that."

"Dad, I thought you always wanted us to be modest about everything. Including looks. I was carrying out your instructions."

"Modest, Mahlon? I could say that you have plenty to be modest about, but I won't."

"Hey Dad, you're no male model yourself."

I had heard enough. "I'll deal with this later, Mahlon. Why didn't Kilion tell me?"

Mahlon stared. "There's lots he doesn't tell you. He knows you have so many sorrows of your own, he's stopped bothering you."

"Is that why you send him to me, Elimelech? Because he won't come on his own account? What kind of a mother have I become?"

Elimelech shook his head and called his younger son who

~ 79 ~

appeared, dabbing at his cheek. He motioned to him to sit down and began.

"Right, let's start with the financials. Income-wise, we're doing better. We're staying in the black. One day we could even look at buying land if this continues. Set up the business. Elimelech and Sons."

Kilion piped up. "Don't forget Mum. She's worked harder than any of us."

"Elimelech and Sons and Mum. Doesn't have a ring to it, if I'm honest."

I piped up. "Have you been refunded for any of either property management agency's failings yet?"

"It's on my list. Now how are we all doing socially? Are we feeling part of the community yet? I am."

I was brutally frank. "I want to go home. I've never been easy in my mind about the Chemosh god business. It's evil. Children have been slaughtered for this. The people around us are generally fine, they're used to us, and the odd one is even friendly nowadays, but their culture is a total no-no for me. We don't belong."

Mahlon looked briefly sympathetic. "It's a generation thing, Mum. Kilion and I quite like it. We've been to a few events now with our Moab peers, and the Chemosh cult doesn't worry them. They do it to keep their parents happy. Anyway, we 've both made a few friends."

Kilion spoke for himself. "If I'm honest, I don't like the ones in my age group who won't talk about anything else than Chemosh. There's a few I don't like. They seem hooked. They do believe in him, or it. But it's good to have real mates."

Mahlon justified his earlier comment. "Yes, the besotted

ones are ok, just a bit lost. They're at a funny age. They'll be fine when they mature. It's adolescence. Exploring their world spiritually as well as materially."

Kilion wasn't so sure. "I think Mum has a point. We should listen to her. These guys seem to justify everything they want to do by saying that Chemosh requires it. They say they must surrender to his will. But to me, it's just a way of legitimising whatever they want to do."

Mahlon was quick to reply. "Kil, most of the kids we know just let the weird ones get on with it. We should just ignore them."

Elimelech nodded. "Yes. And what's more, you two boys need to be looking for a wife each. You need to plan ahead. You won't always have your mum to look after you."

I didn't like my husband's tone of voice. Was it me, or was his frustration pushing him to dark thoughts?

I was relieved when Kilion grinned. "Mahlon's showing me how to talk to girls. He's been doing it ever since we arrived here. He says I need to get rid of my spots."

Elimelech laughed. "How many girls have shown interest in you two?"

Mahlon added gravity to the tone. "It's a work in progress, Dad. It's a marathon, not a sprint. We were foreigners to them for such a long time. But our charm will win the day."

Kilion grimaced. "Not while I'm so spotty. That's what you tell me, bro."

I was pleased that my voice was measured but quiet. "When can we go home? Can't you give me some hope? We shouldn't be here. We should be with our people."

"How many times? Hunger's still the issue, Nomes. Still

the case. A traveller came through town a few days back and he said that the famine shows no sign of ending."

I didn't throw in the fact that Sara's husband had passed through Bethlehem recently and reported that the situation was not quite as simple as Eli wanted us to believe.

It didn't help my case when Mahlon weighed in to support his father. "Mum, we'll do that one day. When Dad says it's time. But for now, we're doing fine. The food's great. You're a good cook, we're earning money. What more could we want?"

Elimelech flashed him a smile. "Seriously? More social opportunities, for a start. Choose a wife each. It takes time, you know."

"Well, as I was saying, Dad, we have to go to the Chemosh Appeasement Ceremonies for that. It clashes with everything we were taught in Bethlehem. But that's okay. Who knows what is true?"

Kilion wasn't so sure. "Some of it is weird. They have a thing about human sacrifice. Human blood is what Chemosh sometimes requires, apparently. The kids we hang out with steer clear of that, but it's always in the background."

I made myself clear. "I told you that. Kilion, that frightens me. You shouldn't go anywhere near it, boys."

Mahlon was for discounting my advice. "Then Dad will be angry as we won't meet any girls. You two need to get your act together, never mind us."

Elimelech straightened in his chair. "Now, now, Mahlon. Enough."

"Sorry, Dad. But don't you need to help Mum to feel accepted now? That initial enmity is over, well over. She obviously doesn't have a sense of belonging. She's not as sparky as she once was. Nothing like."

I sensed my lip trembling. I had never heard Mahlon speak like this, "I'm uneasy, Son. I don't think the hatred is ever far away with some people. Wars are so hard to forgive. The Lord isn't in this place, and we've abused His love by staying here. I get the food problem, Mahlon, but life is about so much more."

Kilion stroked the back of my hand, but it was his brother who broke the short silence. "You're over-worrying, Mum."

I stared at my husband. "Elimelech, don't think I haven't seen them. They're back here every day. Tell me we aren't paying protection money to that security business again."

Elimelech frowned at me. "Hang on Naomi, not in front of the children! What do you mean, the security business? My property management friends? You're getting over-emotional."

I moved directly to the point. "Don't make me even more angry, Elimelech. They are men now. Just consider whether or not they need to hear this. Have you, or have you not, cut your ties with the agency as you promised?"

"Naomi, stop. I'll deal with you later."

Chapter Twelve

The Batten

I gulped and sat back. Mahlon shook his head at his father. "Go on, Mum."

Now was clearly not the moment, but I managed a few words to reassure the boys. "One day, I will, but only when your father permits. Suffice it to say that I think what's happening is not simply down to your father's charms. Something is wrong."

Elimelech took the unclear pathway of the vague. Excluding him from knowing what Sara had done had worked. "At least you all know how safe we are here. There's no denying that the neighbours have been great since we got involved in the community. Time has passed by, and things have changed. Through hard work, we have achieved my aims. If there's a bit of peripheral support, so be it. Don't ever forget, everyone, that our forefathers here did not come in peace. Of course we are going to be the objects of suspicion. There's always costs. That's business. Your mum isn't used to the commercial environment, so she wouldn't understand. I am, so you can trust me."

I had heard enough and moved towards the door. "I just don't want you taken for a fool, Elimelech. We should never have left Bethlehem." I left the room.

I waited behind the door until Elimelech decided on a none-too-confidential whisper. "Boys, your mum doesn't mean this. She's been rather overwrought lately. She's been working too hard."

Kilion decided to speak up for his mother. "She has. To help support us all. She's fearful that we're not seeing the benefit of what we're all doing, because of these business expenses. She had built up her hopes that we were going home, and Dad's just told her we're not. She only has her Lord to turn to, and even he doesn't seem to be interested. No wonder she's not jumping for joy right now."

Mahlon returned to the financials. "Dad, is this right about the security payments?"

Elimelech folded his arms. "Life's not straightforward, Son. You'll find that out."

He was in a strange mood with me. Maybe I was wrong to walk out. That night, there was an incident. I was on my knees, cleaning the door, when part of the wood fell off. It was grotty anyway. I shouted out in frustration, and he stormed downstairs, grabbed the batten and stood over me. I suspected he was about to hit me but stopped when he heard Mahlon's steps.

I said nothing about it the next day, which was no better than its predecessor. Kilion finished his breakfast and looked at me. "Mum, you're looking so sad. Can we change the subject for a while? Talk about the old days again?"

Mahlon shook his head. "I've tried, Kil, but Mum can't."

"Can we just talk about our ancestors again? Who they were, where we come from?" Kilion was hopeful.

My response disappointed him. "Not now."

Kilion sniffed. "It's just that living in a foreign land makes you focus on your heritage."

Elimelech saw I was close to tears. His compassion was legendary. "Boys, this is not the moment. You mother is still angry about yesterday's discussion."

I muttered something barely audible before trying to respond appropriately. "Angry? I'm not angry. My heart is broken. We need to go home to Bethlehem."

I'm genuinely sorry to tell you that Elimelech was drawn in. "That's the bottom line for your mother. She's homesick. I hear her. But we made our move here, and here is where we stay."

I began to sob. No-one came to me, not even Kilion. I managed to raise my voice but not my eyes. "Have you all misunderstood me so badly? That's not fair, even by your father's standards."

Elimelech summed up. "Boys, I don't want a fight over this. I'm going to deal with everything for your mum, so she won't have to worry any more. But with God as my witness, I'm telling you we aren't moving anywhere."

"Come on Dad, can't we just talk about our wider family for a few minutes? We keep asking. Mum would like that."

Right then, I wouldn't. Elimelech closed the discussion. "Sorry, Kilion, that's not going to help. Anyway, I need some time. I'll find the best way of putting an end to everything that bothers your mum. I'm going out for a walk now to clear my head. Any chat about the family will have to wait."

I don't know why I asked, maybe hoping to talk my husband round. "May I come with you, Elimelech?"

He refused flatly. "No. There's nothing more to be said. I'm going alone. You get on with your housework here."

Chapter Thirteen

Molars Bared

Two more years grated by. There were more incidents, of course. Sometimes he resorted to directly vicious verbal assaults, and other times, more subtle. He grew even more secretive about our finances. I felt caged in but stuck it out for my boys. I took it for the team, but it nearly broke me.

Sara was my strongest support. There was always more she needed to know, and I told her about the old times. Where she got her questions from, I do not know, but they kept coming.

One night as I was preparing food, I let it slip that I had a friend. Red rags and bulls don't come into it. Elimelech's face was on fire with rage. He jumped up and set his face an inch from mine. His tone was one which he had never used before, to me at least. He bared his teeth like a threatened animal and spat out each word, making his displeasure crystal clear.

When he finished, he pulled back his arm and clenched his fist. I tensed, waiting for the blow. As he did, Kilion walked in and shouted to Mahlon, who ran downstairs. The shocked boys put themselves between us. Elimelech stormed out of the house, leaving his dignity in the kitchen.

I calmed Mahlon and Kilion down, amazingly. We agreed to tell no-one, and put it down to an illness, or even the stresses of business. We agreed to continue as if it had never happened, although I could see Mahlon's fury in his eyes. I think he would have planted his father one when he returned, if it had been left to him. I was suitably grateful and felt reassured in the moment. But my self-esteem had never been so low, and I have never been able to forget what took place.

I told the boys about Sara, name and all. They were pleased for me and told me that I must carry on that friendship. Elimelech would not know either her name or where we met, they said, and I thought that was so. In his eyes, the marketplace was where I earned my contribution to his finances, so I vowed to be cautious, but to keep the channel open.

It was three hours later when he returned. He wiped the dust from his footwear, closed the door behind him and headed back to the kitchen. "Mahlon, Kilion, come here."

Kilion saw his frown and remembered our agreement. "What's up, Dad?"

Mahlon did likewise. "Hey Dad, who's rattled your cage? Your face looks like you're chewing a lemon."

"I'll come to the point. Cage is about right. This house is getting too small for us. You two are still sharing, and you're grown men. You've got too much stuff. And you eat like camels."

Mahlon attempted humour to further the atmosphere of artificial normality. "Camels in a cage. You've broken the simile. Do you mean quantity or style in terms of food consumption? Or is it the old lecture about manners again?"

Elimelech did not reciprocate. "I'm not in the mood for flippancy, Son."

Kilion sat back. "Are we moving? Can we stay in this town?"

His father held up a hand. "We? There is no 'we'. Nor is there any moving."

Mahlon was on the edge of his chair. "What do you mean, Dad?"

I couldn't believe what he came out with next. "Boys, your mum needs a break. We've known that for a while. She's still not herself."

I coughed. "Why don't you ask me, Elimelech?"

Elimelech didn't answer but looked at our boys. "Listen, it was not that long ago that you assured me you would be finding a girl each, getting married and settling down."

Mahlon was quick to correct him. "Kilion didn't. He was more worried about his spots. And he still is."

Kilion did his bit for normality. He screwed up his nose. "No need for that, Mahlon, no need."

"I'm sure that there was a commitment from you both. I've seen no sign of progress. Spots or no spots, you are both fine looking young men. What's going on?"

"Marathon, Dad, marathon. Not a sprint. We're on the road."

"To nowhere, as far as I can see, Mahlon. It's time you two moved out."

"Not yet, Dad, but Kilion has a new friend. She's called Orpah. He met her at a Chemosh youth placation party. And before Mum asks, she hates the human sacrifice thing."

I wasn't sure I liked where this was heading.

Mahlon appealed to his father. "Dad, you were a teenager once. We can't rush romance. Or moving out."

"Ok, sorry, I'll reboot this conversation. Kilion's new girl is a bit of a looker, right? How did he make this fine catch?"

Mahlon smirked. "Easy, Father, easy. It was me who coached him in how to get her attention."

Elimelech, to my great relief, climbed down further. The crisis had passed, for now. "You coached Kilion in getting a girl's attention? And she's still interested? Amazing."

Kilion winced. Elimelech stared at him. Why couldn't he have left it at the compliment? "Come on Son, how long till the wedding?"

Chapter Fourteen

Responsible Men

My husband's cynical humour was wasted on Mahlon. "Wedding? She only met him yesterday. You're being a bit previous, Dad, if you don't mind my saying so."

"What about you, Mahlon? You're older than him. Put your coaching skills to even better use and get your own life sorted."

"Don't start on me, Dad. Meeting girls requires money. I can't move out to my own place, if that's what you were driving at. A man needs disposable income. I need to splash some cash. You're stuck with me."

I threw in my pennyworth. "Elimelech, we actually need to be talking about going home, not extending our tentacles here."

"That's not going to happen, Nomes, not yet. The famine is ongoing. I'll say one thing about family. And that is that Nonny was right. The Bethlehem weather has changed, and not for the better. So we're staying put. Right, Mahlon?"

"Right by me, Dad, if we stick together and look after mum. Just one thing. How do you gather this information? Bethlehem's a long way from here."

It seemed further than ever. Eli was bluffing. Sara's husband had spent some time in Bethlehem of late, and she updated me regularly. A range of food was available, if at a price.

I spoke up. "I'm sure it's not that bad. Moving back takes the Chemosh culture out of the equation."

"Are you still on that old tack? Move on, woman. Relax. Give up on all that rubbish. They were well taught by the rabbi. Isn't that so, boys?"

I didn't afford either of them the time to respond. "That was years ago. They forget. We all do. Including you, Elimelech."

He didn't concur. "Naomi, I remember whatever is important. And that includes your happiness. I've promised you I'll make things better. It's part of my job as your husband."

Kilion picked up my body language and tried to relieve my sense of doom. "Can't you just tell us about Nonny? What does that name mean? I met him but I've forgotten whatever I knew about the man, or most of the wider family for that matter."

I could see where this might be heading, and my hopes were raised. Could it be a reasoned family discussion about the values of our nation and the Lord who had saved His people from the kind of slavery I now found myself in?

Elimelech appeared to react positively. "I don't get why you keep on about this, Kilion, but if it matters that much, with one proviso, I'll agree. Your mum tells it better than me."

"What's the condition, Dad?"

My heart fell on hearing his response. "That you keep it

simple. About those we left behind, alive. It won't help your mum if you dig over what their Lord did for those who went before. Circumstances are so different. I'm saying this because I have promised to help your mum through the rough patch she's experiencing."

Kilion's reaction was wide-eyed. "Doesn't Mum get a say? And if you're splitting us up by telling Mahlon and me to move out, Dad, I think it should be you who recounts the family story. You seem to be dictating this narrative."

Bless him, he'd tried. He had fought my corner.

His father deflected the jibe. "Son, you'll soon learn for yourself that being a man comes with responsibilities for the women in his care. If you marry your new friend, you'll realise that. We go out into the world. We see the big picture. Running a home doesn't do that. Erm, why's Mum left the room?"

I caught Kilion's expression and welled up. The love of my son was too much for my battered emotions. Nonny would remain anonymous.

Eli didn't notice. "She's probably quite busy. My advice to you is not to interfere."

Kilion was feisty. "I want to hear this. What kind of people do we come from? What qualities do we men have to live up to?"

His father assumed a tone I can only describe as verging on the patronising. "It's all very respectable. Upright and responsible men. That's the core of this family. As you can see with me, Kilion."

Kilion went for it. "Mum's not included then? Or is it all women?"

Elimelech coughed. "All our people are upright and responsible men and, yes, women."

"Ok, Dad. Now remind us of where our respectability comes from. Wasn't there a prostitute in the family? How respectable is that?"

Elimelech waved a hand. "Steady on, Son. Let's not condemn her before we begin. We need to go back some seventy years to find her story."

"Well, Mum is elsewhere in the house, so let's go there. Weren't our people still in the wilderness then?"

Mum was still just round the corner, recovering some composure.

His father theatrically puffed out his chest before another cough denied him the effect he was seeking. "They were. And our great leader Moses had just died, having brought the nation to the edge of the promised land. He's buried somewhere in Moab, apparently. Maybe your mother has forgotten that little detail. Moses didn't ever go home."

Mahlon, who had been listening intently, shrugged diffidently. "I think I remember that from her teaching when we were little. Was that the same Moab as we live in now?"

Eli sounded relieved. Mahlon was a softer target for his rhetoric. "Absolutely, Son. Our people entered Canaan through Moab. We've got history here."

Kilion glanced at his father. "If Moses was buried here like Mum taught us, can we see his grave? It'd feel more like home for Mum."

"No-one knows where the grave is, Kilion. Anyway, the promised land wasn't here, Son. Our true home is the one our people took forty years to find, and which God provided."

On hearing this, I returned to the room. The opportunity was put on a plate. "Your father is right. That's why I wish we could go back there. God provided it for you, Kilion, you, Mahlon, and your parents too."

Kilion stared at me. "One day, you will go home, Mum. Dad can't argue with that. He's just said as much."

This was as far as I'd ever got, and Elimelech knew it. He wiped his forehead. "Let's not be hasty. It won't be just yet. There's some news I haven't told you. When I met those travellers the other day, one of them lingered for a longer chat. He told me he had heard reports of a disease there at the moment as well as the famine. A nasty illness caused by malnutrition. It's killed a few people already."

He was back on shifting sands. Sara hadn't mentioned any fatal outbreaks of illness, but her husband would not necessarily have heard this. I decided to say nothing.

Kilion shuddered. "I hope it's not a plague."

Kilion nodded. "But Dad, you're going off the point. I was asking about our family's lady of the night. Tell us more. Even if Mum's here. She won't want to be catching anything back in Bethlehem if your info is right."

Chapter Fifteen

Hospitality

A look of relief crossed Elimelech's features. "Ok, so before the nation crossed into Canaan, they sent spies ahead to check out what was going on there."

Mahlon interrupted with a grin. "Good plan. And don't tell me, they fancied a bit of…"

He got no further. "Son, I hope you meant supper? Stop right there. I will not have you belittle men who risked their all for you. They needed somewhere to hide for the night."

Mahlon acquiesced. "I was talking about supper. I recall her name, though, It was Rahab. She was a convenient option."

"Mahlon, careful!"

I intervened. "Don't judge, Mahlon."

He didn't. "Rahab was on the other side, wasn't she? She wasn't one of us."

"No, but something, or someone, told her to take them in. She had the space to offer hotel accommodation."

"Hotel, Dad? I think we know what kind of hotel Rahab ran!"

"Forget that thought now, Mahlon. God was moving in her heart."

"Mum, does God really care for prostitutes? But aren't they dirty? Don't they break a commandment or two? They're not the kind of person we would want in our town, are they?"

I'd said my piece and was enjoying Eli's discomfort. "I'll let your father continue. Let's hear it from him."

To me, Elimelech hid a feeling of suspicion and was slightly cagey. "The story goes that Rahab sheltered them, kept them safe. So, when they left her place in Jericho to go back across the river, the pressure was on her as well as them."

Mahlon whistled. "I can't remember. Was she found out, Dad?"

"No, Son, that's the thing. They escaped via a window. The climbed down a red scarf of hers."

Mahlon stopped him. "Ah yes, it's all coming back to me. They must have made strong scarves in those days. Perhaps a gift from a grateful…"

I saved his blushes. "Guest? They went one at a time."

Mahlon's expression twinkled. "The spies or Rahab's guests?"

I smiled inwardly but held the line. "Your father has warned you about flippancy, Son. It is inappropriate."

Mahlon returned the affection. "Sorry Mum, I can't help myself. Wasn't the scarf the signal to the Israelite soldiers that they weren't to harm her during the actual battle?"

"Good knowledge, Son. She had to display the scarf in the window. She was a heroine for our people."

Mahlon hadn't finished. "And a traitor to her own. I guess

she was top of their 'wanted' list. There'd be a death warrant out on her."

Elimelech rejoined the narrative. "Boys, she wasn't safe among her own people anymore, so ours adopted her. And she met a man she liked."

Mahlon grinned at his mother. "Was that unusual in her line of business?"

I hadn't felt uplifted like this for a very long time. Both boys were doing my work for me. "You make me laugh, Mahlon. She met a good man by the name of Salmon. What's the matter with you, Kilion?"

"Salmon? That sounds a bit…"

"…fishy? That's an old one, little bro."

"Boys, stop being so tiresome. Do you want the rest of the story or not? Your mother hasn't got all day." Elimelech sounded irritated.

Mahlon hadn't finished. "Sorry Dad. I do know my plaice. Pray continue."

Whatever humour he still had in his life seemed to have abandoned him. "That's quite enough of your mockery."

Mahlon apologised, and after a moment, Eli resumed the account. "So, Salmon married Rahab. He made an honest woman of her, and they had a son. His name was Boaz. You know him as Uncle Boaz."

The man he had described as boring was now fascinating, but Kilion had seen another issue. "Hang on, so our great grandma was not of our race?"

His father shook his head. "No. She was a refugee. And a fine woman. Don't you forget that."

I agreed. "Yes. May I add something?"

Elimelech was theatrically effusive. "Of course, my dear. You must feel very strongly about Rahab."

This was not my point. "I admire her, but it's not that. It's just that two generations above you boys in this family, there was a migrant without whom neither of you boys would have been here."

Elimelech thought he'd spotted his moment. "And Moab was involved. Being here now brings home what those family members went through to settle us down."

I pounced. "Exactly. Settled in Bethlehem. So I ask again and without hope of an answer from you, when are we going back there, Eli? Moses may be buried here, but our place is clearly back in Bethlehem. These boys would be much better off trying to find suitable Israelite girls, not Moabites."

Eli held out the palms of his hands. "I'll give you a promise. We'll be done here in two years' time, Naomi. Surely the famine will be over by then."

Chapter Sixteen

Chest Pains

We stayed on, of course. Little more was ever said about moving house, other than Eli maintaining that the boys should stand on their own two feet. I saw the flipside, being me, and concluded that our finances were still not in good order. Surely by now, we should have been able to fund a part of their move to independent living. But we never got there.

Some months in, I was chatting as usual with Sara as I unenthusiastically touted my wares. She told me her husband had revisited Bethlehem and had arrived back feeling under the weather. His forehead was warm to the touch, and she had cared for him with water and honey. He was not a well man.

I offered to help. She refused initially, but I insisted on walking back with her part way to her home. It was a risk. Eli remained unaware that I had her friendship and would have been furious to catch me. Sara was my friend, whilst Eli was a remote, cold figure whom I had once loved. He had killed our relationship in any meaningful way.

She stopped me some way from reaching her home, probably because the neighbours wouldn't want to see her associating with a migrant. In the distance, I saw a fine home with their camel tethered to the gate. To say the beast was run down would imply that it had once blossomed and flourished in a glorious era in life, and I couldn't see that being the case. It had not seen better days. She smiled and told me that they just used it locally.

The following day, she brought me a gift. It was a lovely gesture, I thought, a kind of pick-me-up potion, with some honey. I wondered if she feared she had passed on her husband's affliction to me, and was ensuring I didn't suffer. Either way, it was a kindness.

Nothing developed with me over the following forty-eight hours, as it happened, and she seemed fine too. We both seemed to be symptom-free.

However, I had to call out for help early the next morning. "Kilion? Mahlon? Are you there? Can you come quickly? Your dad's really not right."

Kilion was first to respond. He yawned. "Right? He's always right. Just ask him."

"Kilion, I'm not joking. He's had a terrible night. I've given him some honey and a local medicine I came by. I'm hoping it helps."

"Mum, is it like that cough he gets occasionally? That has its moments, but he gets through."

"No, Son. He's struggling to catch his breath. It's more like a panic attack. He's had a few recently, but this is bad. Is Mahlon there?"

"No, Mum, he went out at first light. He's been doing that for months now to avoid annoying Dad. I've got a bit of time. Can I help?"

"See, he's very pale."

"Poor Dad. These kinds of sicknesses are devastating for older people. All the locals here are blaming Israel for starting the most recent one. They say it's been brought here by travellers."

"And what do the travellers say?"

"They say it's divine punishment."

"The Lord has plenty of reasons to punish our nation, Kilion."

"Mum, are you saying that Dad's done wrong? And what if some people really have died of it? Where does that leave us? Is God sending us pestilence?"

"Kilion, let's focus on your dad. I'll give him food and water. And hope for the best."

"Come on Mum, you've forgotten something. We will pray for him."

"His chest pains bother him more and more. Kilion. He seems to have so much anxiety of late. But yes, good lad, of course we should, and we will, pray."

"Mum, the pressure Dad seems to feel is why Mahlon steers clear. He doesn't want to add to the problem. Dad made it clear when he promised the two-year plan that he wanted us out of the house as soon as possible, and it hasn't happened. We've got nowhere to go. Is it our fault he's so stressed? We did try, Mum, but he never had the money to back us up."

"All I know, Son, is that underneath it all, he loves you both. But something's badly wrong. Will you pray with me now?"

"I will, later, yes. I can't just now. I'm going over to see Orpah, Mum. I pray with her sometimes."

"To the Lord? That's good. I knew you'd turn out well."

"Not exactly. We pray to both. To our God and hers. Hers is Chemosh. She's attached to him, in a moderate kind of way. I'm only respecting her culture."

"Promise me again you won't become part of it, Son. Remember who you are, and who your God is."

"Our God isn't doing great right now, Mum. Just look at Dad. And you're not in great shape."

My tone intensified. "You don't understand, do you? You still want God to do what you want. Our Lord does what he sees as the best. There's a difference!"

Kilion waved. "Got to dash. I'm meeting her folks. They have invited me to go to one of their appeasement-discerning conferences next weekend. I've said okay. Mahlon's coming too."

"What about your dad? This is hardly good timing, Kilion."

"He'll pull through. I'm sure you and God can take care of him. I'll help more when we get back."

"Why is Mahlon going with you, may I ask?

Chapter Seventeen

Fading

"Orpah has a friend called Ruth. Mum, he's hopeless at getting girls. Clueless. Orpah wants us to set them up. Ruth's a bit quiet, but he'll like that."

Kilion left the house. I heard Eli coughing in the bedroom but was planted into my chair by a dark thought. Had I inadvertently passed on an illness? If Sara was asymptomatic, could I be too? Two days of torment beckoned.

The time passed so slowly, broken only by one very unexpected visitor. No-one else called, but why should they? My boys were away, apparently appeasing Chemosh. I isolated myself from Eli as far as possible. He started leaving his meals uneaten. I had no choice but to go in. "Eli, I need to speak to you, I'm coming in. You've left your food again. You need strength to fight this off."

Elimelech struggled to sit up. "I know. I'll keep trying. I did drink the medication you gave me, but I'm not sure it has helped."

I smiled. "It will. Now there's something I need to know. Please be honest with me."

"What is it?" Even as a sick man, he was giving no promises of truth.

"One of those protection men was outside earlier, asking for you. They've never done that before. What's happening, Eli?"

My husband attempted a deep breath and winced with the effort. "Things aren't what they were with them. They kept me against my will for an hour last week. It was quite frightening. Nomes, I've realised that I'm not as young as I was."

This may have been true, if incomplete. I pursed my lips. "Then they'll get the illness too. I hope the bloke who came here was there when they called. Look, why did they seize you, other than to make you poorly?"

"They're increasing the charge for their services, that's all."

"Did you give them money?"

"No. We don't have enough to do so."

My face turned pale. "No!"

Elimelech sank back on his bed. His voice dropped. "My chest is hurting more and more. I don't know how much more of this I can take. It's worse after the medication, I'm sure."

I knew what I had to do. "I'm going to pray. To the Lord."

I leave him a couple of hours before returning to the bedroom. He was lying still, then painfully managed to turn his head slightly towards me. "Nomes, it's getting worse. My lungs hurt when I breathe. My stomach is churning."

I sounded almost stoical. "Keep fighting, Eli, keep fighting. I'll get you something to eat."

His voice was little more than a whisper. "Tell the boys I love them."

"I can't right now. They're at the Chemosh affair. They'll be back Monday. You tell them then."

"I think you'll have to do it for me."

From somewhere came a phrase I hadn't said for a very long time. Tears filled my eyes. "I love you, Eli." Despite everything, I meant it.

He cried too. "We should never have come to Moab. It's all my fault."

My heart melted. "You did what you thought was right, Eli. That's all. Just one thing. Have you been paying them money all this time?"

His sobbing was audible. "Pray for me, Nomes. Forgive me."

I had to pause. A confusion of thoughts tumbled from my lips. "Eli, sometimes I wonder if God is even listening. Being here has crippled me, and I've been angry. With you and with God. I'll pray if I can, of course I will. I do forgive you."

Eli made one last effort before his body fell limp. His eyes flickered briefly. "Thank you, Nomes. Tell the boys."

Like Moses, we buried him in Moab. I went back to the house, shaken numb by the finality of bereavement. I was in turmoil, yet again.

Back in my chair, I discerned a knock on the door. The boys weren't due back till the next day, so who could it be? I dreaded it being another security operative, but my fears were unfounded. My unexpected visitor was Sara.

~ * ~ * ~

She looked around her before coming in, then folded her arms around me like never before. I clung to her hug until she pulled away, checking nervously all around. No-one saw us. Her husband had recovered, she said. The disease had left him. As she moved to the door, she asked if she could return one day soon. She had something to tell me when her husband was away.

The next day, I looked onto the street and saw my younger son returning. I opened the door and waited. My voice trembled with emotion. "Come in, Kilion. I'm so glad you're back."

Kilion knew nothing but was bubbling with excitement. I couldn't stop him. "Mum, it was a really good weekend. We both had a great time. There were some great people there and the music was out of this world. Mahlon had a fantastic time, and he's got some news."

I managed a brief smile. "Kilion, I'm glad. But something's happened here. And it's not good."

Kilion looked at her quizzically. "Mum? Are you okay? You look grey! You didn't develop symptoms too? Are you feeling ill? Can I go and get the doctor for you? I don't suppose Dad could have done much to help in his condition."

"Kilion, sit down. I have some very bad news. He's dead."

"My dad?" He clutched my open arms as the tears rolled. He babbled uncontrollably. "Please, no. I didn't get to say goodbye. Are you okay? Did the neighbours help?"

"They helped bury him, that's all. Everyone's probably scared of the illness. It's not like we've got family to rely on. And we're still seen as foreign."

Kilion partially recovered his poise for his mum's sake.

"They've made your life a misery, Mum, if we're honest. Was there anything else?"

I winced. "There was. You remember Dad's security men?"

"The ones he thought were our friends. That's who you mean?"

"Yes. Although calling them friends was for our benefit, as you probably worked out. They were pressuring your dad again over increasing the payments. That led to panic attacks."

"They're like a big health warning, right? That makes sense. They call it an underlying condition. Poor Dad."

"I guess so. Look, Kil, I have to share this. I may have been responsible for his death."

"You, Mum? No way. There's not a grain of malice in you. What on earth are you talking about?"

I told him about Sara, her husband and the affliction. "Mum, you didn't know."

"Have I been foolish, Kilion? Tell me!"

"Mum, you've been blaming yourself for everything that has gone wrong for the last ten years. If Dad had listened to you, he wouldn't have ever been here. How can that be down to you?"

I told him about Eli's last words. "He died knowing I loved him. He wanted my forgiveness. I gave it to him, although I still have to process it."

Kilion glanced out of the window. "Mahlon will be here soon. He thinks he's bringing Ruth to meet you both. I'll head him off. It's not the time for introductions."

I didn't want that. Mahlon needed to come home too.

"Don't do that, Kilion. Dad's in a good place. No more pain. No more threats."

"If you're sure. Everything is happening so fast. Dad, and Mahlon."

"Mahlon? Why? What's happened to him?"

"Mum, it was like love at first sight. They spent all day talking together. About God. Chemosh and our God. Ruth was fascinated. Kept questioning him about the Lord. She's hooked."

"Kilion, what about Orpah. What did she think?"

"She loved it. Said they were made for each other. She said we were too. Mum, I wanted Dad's blessing. We're going to get married next month. The same day as Mahlon and Ruth."

My jaw hit the floor. I eventually managed a few words. "You two don't hang around. Dad would want to know you were both happy. And he would want our God's blessing on you too, never mind hers."

Kilion nodded. "Obviously, with what's just happened, we'll allow all the time we need to mourn Dad first, Mum. We'll leave things a while. Mahlon will want nothing else."

Chapter Eighteen

Extremists

Kilion had been out looking for his brother to break the news of Elimelech's death, and on their return, Mahlon's expression betrayed the shock of the event.

I glanced up briefly on hearing his footsteps. He reached down to embrace me. "It's okay, Mum. I'm back. You're not dealing with this alone."

I squeezed his arm but could find no words. He tried again. "Mum, you, Kilion and I are a team. We'll protect you. We'll take care of you. Don't worry."

Two weeks dragged by. The shock of Eli's passing was still intense, and my sense of engagement in daily life was vague, like being in a bad dream. Nagging away at the back of my mind were Sara's words, but I hadn't been back to the market. I needed to know what she had to tell me but found myself afraid in case it was something radically scary.

I had diverted my thoughts by asking a question of my younger son. "Kilion, you seem preoccupied. What's on your mind? I know it's been a whirlwind, but since the festival, something's been bothering you. Is it your dad? Or is it Orpah?"

Kilion sniffed. "No, Mum, not them. I wanted to talk to you when I got back, but it wasn't the time, and I'm not sure it is now."

"I'm listening, Son. Go ahead."

"There was this radical group who called themselves the ultras. They were speaking out about Chemosh requiring more sacrifices. And urgently. And they didn't mean animals. People were listening to them. I'd hate for that to spread. But I fear it's going to."

"That's not good, Kilion. Not good at all."

"Mum, some of them were from round here. I think they knew Dad."

"Hang on a minute. You say that they don't want animal sacrifices. What do they want?"

"Human sacrifice, Mum. But they want to carry out a purge. Clean up Chemosh's following. Purify the believers. Human blood was required to be spilled. I was scared."

"I'm not surprised, Kilion. But we aren't supporters of Chemosh, the Lord is our God. Our God is one of power, Chemosh is an evil spirit."

"That's not the point, Mum. Mahlon and I were both seen at the conference. We are foreigners. They know who we are and they know where we live."

"Am I being naïve? Surely, they'd be pleased. They want to spread their cult. Surely, they'd see foreign followers as a trophy?"

"No. You don't get it. We are outsiders. We are dirty in their eyes because of who we are, and they're into cleansing. Don't forget the war between us was their grandparents' conflict, so some of them still hate us for that. We're in real danger."

I attempted to bring calm. "You're still in shock, Son. Look, Ruth and Orpah being on the scene will mean it won't happen. Both are fine young women. You boys have a great future. Let's talk about it tonight. We can talk weddings too."

Kilion smiled. "I don't know how you do it. You're a wonderful lady, Mum. I need some of your peace. How can you think about weddings so soon after we lost Dad? You're talking like you've just found some amazing kind of peace!"

"It's not mine, Kilion. It belongs to God, and he can give you it. I used to enjoy it before we left our own people in Bethlehem. It's around me over your dad. I just hope it lasts."

"He's real to you, the Lord, isn't he? But he doesn't seem to stop you grieving, Mum."

"Kilion, I am deeply saddened. But at this moment, I know it's the Lord who has enabled me to carry on. Even when reality strikes and I hit rock bottom. Your dad's gone, and soon you'll be gone to create your own families. The Lord is my rock."

Kilion shook his head sadly. "And in those times, do you still feel that peace, Mum?"

"I'd be untruthful if I told you that was so. When I lose it, I start thinking about what I could do for my future. And I can't get beyond not having one. Kilion, I'm not even sure I could go home. In my darkest moments, it feels as if the Lord has abandoned me here without hope."

"Mum! Those words are not from the mother I knew!" Kilion hugged her. "Mahlon and I won't ever abandon you, of course we won't. Never!"

I took the hand proffered by my younger son. My older son followed suit. I paused before raising my eyes to look at them.

"Boys, I know your hearts are sincere, but I'm old enough and wise enough to know that that is not what happens in reality. Your father set a future course for you, and that course wasn't planned with me in mind. I didn't stop him. Your home will be here in Moab. I can't live in this house for fear of harassment, and you will have your own wives and children to defend."

Mahlon motioned to her to stop. "Ruth and I...."

I managed a weak smile which hid my sense of resignation to my fate. "You sound like you're married already."

"What I was going to say, Mum, is that Ruth and I want to talk with you about your God, so we could all understand better. Can we do that?"

"I'm not sure I'm the best person to do that, Mahlon, right now. I frequently feel He has forgotten me. Anyway, you know all that the rabbi taught you, when we lived in Bethlehem. Can't you use that knowledge?"

"Mum, the rabbi taught us a lot of history and of facts. Ruth says it seems like you lived it out. She says that's what we need to hear."

Kilion smiled. "I'll bring my Orpah to that. She may need to listen to you too, Mum. But only when you're ready."

Chapter Nineteen

Stepping Out of Line

It was a few weeks later. I'd finally ventured out, despite the turmoil within over Eli's death. I saw Sara. She hugged me again and repeated her intention to speak together later. There was a new warmth in her eyes, I thought, but maybe I was imagining it. In the state I was in, who could tell?

Back home, Mahlon was in the kitchen with me. He put away the bowl I had just cleaned before turning to me with a smile. "Mum, Ruth and Orpah are calling shortly. We've got time to chat, if you are up for it. You've seemed brighter lately. Am I right?"

"You and Kilion have been so helpful, Mahlon. Your dad would have been proud of you. I'm still surrounded by sadness and guilt, but let's talk. Who knows what it might bring. I'm happy to discuss matters with the four of you."

"Are you sure? I don't want to cause you more torment than you're dealing with now."

I summoned up all the positive energy I had. "You won't. I've enjoyed meeting them over recent weeks. If they have to be Moabites as your father insisted, these two are the best I could hope for. You've both chosen well."

Ten minutes later, the five of us were established around the kitchen table. "Kilion, will you get that little statue from your room, please." My voice was barely more than a whisper.

Kilion patted Orpah's knee, stood up and looked at me. His was nothing like a whisper. "Why do that, Mum?"

I was decisive. "It's important to see what we're talking about."

Mahlon played the diplomat. "We must respect Chemosh, Mum, shouldn't we?"

I returned the compliment, albeit vaguely, and smiled warmly at the two girls. "We should respect the opinions of his followers."

Kilion returned with the ornament. I placed it in the centre of the table, then took the lead. "Ruth, Orpah, what does the name of this statue mean?"

It was Ruth who responded first. "Chemosh? Chemosh means destroyer, Naomi. A powerful destroyer."

"So, I guess you fear him. You, Orpah and all his followers. Right?"

"Yes. As children we are taught that. He can be pretty scary."

"This little statue does that? He looks rather fragile right here."

"We have those to remind us of his power, Naomi. It makes us behave better if we have his constant threat."

"So why do you invest in Chemosh? Can I ask you, Orpah?"

"I don't really know, Naomi. Probably to keep him in a good mood, you know, well disposed towards us. You'd have to ask the leaders really."

"Do you think fear is an appropriate emotion to feel when you contemplate Chemosh as your god, Orpah? Is there genuine respect?"

"Ruth's better at answering questions. She thinks more than me. I just do what I'm told."

"Orpah, don't worry, lots of people are like that. Ruth, what's your take on fear?"

"There's no element of respect in the Chemosh cult, Naomi. You seem to have a different motivation."

I moved my gaze to the boys. "May I check one point, Mahlon and Kilion? Is this an exercise in making me feel better? Have you two put the girls up to this?"

They stared at each other, but it was Ruth who answered. "No, Naomi. It was me. I asked to get to know you more. The more I heard from Mahlon about you and your principles, the way you lived your life, the more I needed to find out. Will you tell me about your God? What's His name?"

I was staggered. "I will, Ruth. His name is a bit complicated, but I'll explain."

Ruth's smile broadened. "Kilion tells me you've struggled a lot. Your God must be quite something if you still believe now."

Kilion turned a shade of beetroot before recovering his poise and steering the conversation to less controversial ground. "Dad's name was important, wasn't it, Mum?"

"Yes, names are, as you well know. His meant 'My God is King'. Remember?"

Ruth was not for turning. "In Moab, we fear Chemosh. Do you fear your God, Naomi?"

"He's almightily powerful, Ruth. It's right to fear him."

Ruth made her point. "If you've gone through all that you have, and are still facing, it can't be as simple as being scared."

"Exactly, Ruth. I cling to the fact that my God is like a father, and I am one of His own. Some say we should be like His children. It's been hard recently, but deep down, I agree with them."

"Naomi, does fear equal respect, then? Is it the same thing? It's not with Chemosh, I tell you!"

"You're a bright spark, young lady. No, Ruth. It's more complex. I'll explain another time when it's just you and me."

Mahlon took his opportunity. "Ruth, everyone is allowed to worship who they want, right?"

It was his mother who replied. "Yes, Mahlon. But Ruth is seeing a bigger picture. Faith must be an informed decision, not a baseless judgement. After all, it's the biggest decision of your life."

Kilion glanced nervously at Orpah. "So, Mum, it's okay to ask questions, even if you've been brought up to worship other gods?"

I needed no second invitation. "It's vital. Doing things because your parents did them is an easy solution, but only if they were right."

Ruth sensed her friend's discomfort. "It's hard to break out from a culture, isn't it, Orpah?"

"It is. What will the family think of you for even asking those questions? That's what is bothering me."

I could only empathise. "That's a tough one to face. It's a brave person who steps out of line first."

Orpah was hesitant. "I'm sure stepping out of line from your own family is brave, but it might be considered foolish. After all, you are rejecting all you have ever learned. All your past."

Ruth acknowledged Orpah's point before countering with one of her own "But if your family truly love you, they should support you. I'm right, aren't I?" She stared at me for approval.

I didn't disappoint her. "I like you, Ruth. True love is rich and precious. Sometimes others follow you when you break ranks."

Orpah raised her hand. "And sometimes they don't. You don't want to be on your own the rest of your life, do you? And what if Chemosh decides to destroy you? That's scary."

Ruth's expression was one of love. "Orpah, I'm not sure the real God would exist on fear alone. Life has fear, death, and tragedy as well as happiness, joy and love. Orpah, we need to think carefully about what Naomi says."

I finally picked up the statue from the table. "Orpah, I believe in the only true God. My God speaks. Look at this statue. Does it speak?"

Orpah screwed up her face. "It's a statue, of course it doesn't speak."

"So does Chemosh communicate anything?"

Orpah was on the ropes. "No-one knows. Not for sure. Powerful people say what Chemosh wants and others follow them."

I shrugged. "What's the point of a god who doesn't speak?

Where's your evidence that Chemosh is powerful? Did Chemosh create the world he now appears to want to destroy?"

Orpah's voice was quieter but betrayed obstinacy. "No. I've never been taught that about him. What's that got to do with it?"

I must have looked incredulous. "My God speaks through creation; that's why it is relevant. He speaks it into being. And he loves what he has made. It's critical."

I turned to Ruth, who had a question. Several, in fact. "Why do things go wrong? Did Mahlon's dad really spend all his money on security? Why were all your belongings ransacked? Why did Mahlon's dad die?"

These were the questions on my own heart, ones which I prayed would be answered one day. Right now, I couldn't help her, but I knew one thing. So I placed a hand on her shoulder. "Ruth, my love, it's the same reason as why my God made the world in love. He gives his creations freedom of choice. It's the most practical part of loving someone truly. We all yearn for freedom, and He gives it us."

Ruth put her hand on top of mine. "Wow. What about the bad things, though? Where do they fit in?"

"Well, God's word tells us that humans took their freedom and made the wrong choices. They took the gift and rejected the giver. So, they broke the relationship, and with it, the creation."

Orpah bounced back. "So, you are saying that what we see now is a damaged world, right? At least Chemosh followers are taught how to behave. Humans need fear in my book. What is your God doing about that? Nothing, from what I can see. Look at what has happened to you and your boys, Naomi."

I took a deep breath. "He's working through his plan to save his people. The ones who listen and choose him. He's got it covered."

Ruth threw a quick glance at Orpah. "He wouldn't be much of a god if he didn't."

It was Orpah's turn to shrug. "Kilion tells me you've suffered for a very long time, Naomi. I can't see how any loving god would put you through all that."

"Kilion's been a star, Orpah, and I can't deny that my faith has been severely tested. None of this is easy. But like our ancestors, we have to try to live our lives trusting him, because he loves us. My God saved my people from something worse than I have experienced. Slavery in a foreign land."

Orpah looked blank. "Kilion and I…"

Mahlon grinned. "Sounds like a wedding speech too. Anything you need to tell us?"

Ruth stepped in. "It does not. Naomi and I…." She paused for effect.

Mahlon stared. "Eh?"

Ruth took a moment before continuing. "…will talk some more when we get a chance."

I laughed. I loved these kids. "We've said most of it just now, Ruth. All I was going to tell you privately. But explaining my beliefs to you has given me a feeling of purpose. I haven't felt like this for years. In fact, since we left Bethlehem."

Mahlon hadn't mentioned the speech for no reason. "Mum, can we talk weddings now?"

Ruth and Orpah sat back as I feigned surprise. "Weddings? Plural? Kilion, what on earth is your brother talking about?"

Kilion grinned. "What about bringing our families altogether for one big celebration? A mega job. Two weddings for the price of...."

I returned his smile. "...of two weddings. There's always at least one extra zero on the bill when they know it's a wedding."

Ruth was reassuring. "Just try and stop us! Naomi, leave it to Orpah and me. Four weeks today and we'll be celebrating. You just have to turn up."

Kilion was serious. "The question is, which God will be blessing our wedding? Does Chemosh even do blessings?"

Ruth was diplomatic. "More like immunity. We'll respect everyone's right to choose, as Mahlon says, but there's only one answer for me."

Orpah shook her head. "The culture will expect otherwise, Ruth. We have to follow the trend."

Ruth smiled. "Orpah, we have to find a way. Naomi, let's make a date to talk more."

Chapter Twenty

Brides

Those four weeks were a time of severe mental trauma, if I'm straight with you. I prayed, of course, but didn't detect any response. It just dragged on. Then I began to experience despair. I despaired of Elimelech for what he'd brought onto me. The boys lifted me, naturally, but I knew I was sinking as soon as they left. Did I hate Eli? I'd like to tell you I didn't, but I was building a ceiling of resentment, turning my pit into an enclosed hell. I couldn't tell anyone. I kept myself indoors. Sara called twice, but I hid. Part of me didn't want a way out. I knew it was all my fault, and I would pay the penalty my way.

The weddings day dawned. It took every ounce of my ability to fake happiness, but I played the part, knowing it was for a short time.

I saw both the brides, beautiful, stunning. I remembered how to show that on my face and muttered a compliment.

Kilion heard it. "Glad you liked it, Mum. I wish Dad was here to see this."

I made a good fist of a smile. "So do I, Son." I didn't feel that at all.

"Mum, maybe he is, in a way. He'd be proud of us standing up for our God."

I shuffled before answering. "I'd like to think so, Kilion." I couldn't tell him of the bitterness in my soul.

He sensed it. "Mum, a few weeks back, you spoke about the Lord in a way you did when we were kids back in Bethlehem. You haven't done that for so long. It got me thinking. Now, I'm ashamed I even gave Chemosh a thought. I'm sorry for putting you through all my doubts."

I struggled for words. "Kilion, you may have found the truth." That was as eloquent as I could manage.

What he said reduced me to more tears. He took my arm. "Mum, the Lord found me. That's what it feels like. I was telling Orpah's family about my journey of faith just now."

Somehow, I felt even worse about myself. Had I doubted that God was in this with me? I had. Did I still? Probably. I managed a question. "How did they take it?"

Kilion moved and took my hand. "Mum, they listened politely. Most of them. Mahlon came over and added his opinions. Ruth stood there with him smiling and nodding. It was a lovely moment."

Anxiety overwhelmed me. This was dangerous. "What did Mahlon say? Was he helpful?"

"Let's say he tried to be diplomatic. It wasn't the best, but I could see what he was trying to do."

"And what about the ones who weren't interested? What did they do?"

"When they worked out what I was talking about, they went off into a huddle."

I understated my feelings. "Does that not bother you, Son?"

Kilion's grin and subsequent answer did nothing for me. "Mum, it's the best day of my life. Nothing can spoil it. Anyway, my Orpah went over to them."

I had to get out of the situation. I'd spotted Sara was there. Was that her husband? His face was covered, but I felt like I'd seen this man before. I had to give her a wide berth, of course. Nor would it have helped if I'd just wandered off, as the boys would have seen me go. I was desperate, so I tried the only angle I could think of. "Kil, I wonder if Ruth can spare me five minutes. I think I need some fresh air."

"I'll get her for you, Mum. She loves you. She'll enjoy a stroll through the village before the dancing really gets going."

Ruth was lovely with me. She talked intensely as we walked, arm in arm. She knew instinctively where I was at, and I loved her deeply for that. She was the daughter I never had. Maybe she would be my salvation, in Moab.

Half an hour later, Ruth put her hand to her ear. "Mum, we'll go back now. They should have started the music. Perhaps they're waiting for us."

I stopped. "One minute, Ruth. Look! Do you know those men? Why are they running across that field?"

"I've seen them somewhere. One of them especially. Aren't they the ones your husband knew in the town, you know, from the property management agency here? Mahlon pointed them out to me when we went to that festival. They were there too."

"My dear, they are not good news. I suspect they helped make our lives a misery. Why do you think they are running?"

Ruth recognised another figure approaching at speed.

"Let's ask Orpah. She's racing towards us now. Something's wrong."

Orpah was breathless. "Come quickly, both of you. They've been attacked."

Ruth grasped my arm. "Who, Orpah? Who has been attacked? Tell us!"

"Your boys. Our husbands. Mahlon and Kilion. They've been stabbed."

I spluttered. "What? Why? Where? What did they do, Orpah?"

"Nothing I could see. They were so happy. Two Bethlehem boys together celebrating marriage. Then I heard chanting and shouting, led by a man who had hidden his face. Next thing, Mahlon and Kilion were down. It was brutal. Then they raced away from the scene." Orpah began to sob.

Ruth drew Orpah to us. Ruth's tone was calm and gentle. "Where are they, Orpah? Let's get them some help."

Orpah shook her head as she cried uncontrollably. "They're dead. They've been murdered."

Ruth collapsed to the ground. Orpah cushioned her head with her hands, babbling desperately. People rushed towards us. It was two days before Ruth spoke again. I had no emotion left to show. I went home and lay still for hours on end, sleepless and without hope. My Kilion, my Mahlon. Both gone.

Her family brought Ruth to my door, along with Orpah. I dragged myself up to greet them. Then they left the three of us together.

We stared at the floor for what seemed like hours, but it was really a matter of minutes.

Finally, I found the courage to speak. "Do they know who did this awful thing? Why? Who could want to ruin so much happiness?"

Orpah winced. "Naomi, people are saying that it was that group from town, the ones you and Ruth saw running away. We know their leader had his face covered. He had the knife, they say. He and his accomplices were shouting that Chemosh had demanded that they destroy these men as a blood sacrifice."

"Were they so offended by the Lord that they had to do this, Orpah?"

"Chemosh is said to be a jealous god."

"Do all his followers do this kind of thing?"

"Naomi, these people were radicalised. Genuine Chemosh adherents would never act in this way. Typically, they toe the party line but keep a low profile. It's a cultural thing. When they see extremists acting in their name, they are horrified. Then they lower their profile even further. Self-preservation."

Ruth had been deep in thought until she heard that. "These criminals claim a supernatural legitimacy for the darkest side of human nature. This wasn't any kind of religious sacrifice. This was senseless slaughter. Racist murder. Am I right, Orpah?"

"People can't say too much, but there's a whisper about another motive. Naomi, Kilion related some of Elimelech's troubles with money, but did you ever fear an escalation of this nature? Was there a vendetta against your family?"

My fears were justified, if these rumours were true. "My husband dealt with them. There were all sorts of payments made. He wouldn't tell me what was going on. Orpah, I just knew something was seriously wrong."

"Are we talking blackmail, Naomi?"

"A protection racket, that's what I suspected."

"So didn't they go for you once your husband passed away?"

"Mahlon and Kilion saw to it that I was safe."

"Could they have taken over the payments without you knowing, Naomi?"

"Mahlon and Kilion? No way. They don't earn enough." She gulped. "I mean they didn't earn enough."

Orpah snapped her fingers. "There's the motive."

Ruth was not so sure. "Revenge? For defaulting on payments? Killing them was a sure way of ensuring they would never get any money ever again. So why do that?"

Orpah spread her hands wide. "Maybe Mahlon and Kilion's murder was to show what happened to anyone who didn't cough up."

I turned pale. "If you're right, Orpah, this is all my fault."

Chapter Twenty-One

A Future Hope

Orpah gritted her teeth. "I want to find them and kill them for what they've done to us."

I begged her not to do that. "No, Orpah, enough evil has been done."

Ruth agreed. "It has, Naomi. Somehow, we all have to rise above this. It wasn't your fault. Never in a million years. I'm as angry as you, Orpah, but let's not do anything hasty."

"I'm blazing with anger, Ruth. Just look at what they've ruined for us all. They've taken all the love from our lives."

I calmed her. "Ruth's right. We need to grieve, Orpah, but just causing someone else to suffer what we're going through isn't going to achieve anything."

"At the moment it feels like it would make me feel a lot better. What can we do, then?"

Ruth added her voice. "Tell us, Naomi, anything."

"Will you girls pray with me tonight? We need to bring this day to God and seek his comfort, and his will, before we do anything. Then we can talk tomorrow."

We prayed together for around an hour. There was lots of

silence. Ruth and I spoke more than Orpah, who found it a little strange. Was there some solace in uniting like this? Perhaps so.

The following afternoon had brought quiet to the street. In my few lighter moments, I'd found a need to ensure my daughters-in-law could find the beginnings of a path to closure.

I was given the strength to welcome the girls back brightly and then made my first point. "Orpah, Ruth, come in. Orpah, tell me you haven't set any revenge in motion."

"No, Naomi, but I hate the people who did this even more than I did yesterday. Have you had an answer to our prayers last night?"

I nodded. "In a way, yes. I hate what they have done. They have taken your husband, and Ruth's, and my sons. But since praying, I can't hate them."

"What?"

"There's something you don't know, Orpah. There have been times since my own husband died, and I went over all he had done to me. As our marriage progressed, his love for me turned to frustration, then to anger, then to physical threats. I was overwhelmed with negativity and dark emotions, which have stayed with me."

The girls were stunned. "Do either of you know what my name means? Naomi means sweetness. So, I prayed cynically to the Lord. I told him to take my name away and give me one which meant how I was feeling. Utterly bitter."

"And how did your God answer you?"

"You walked into my life, with Ruth. You both asked about my faith in the Lord. Suddenly, he was alongside me. He came to carry this awful burden of bitterness with me. It was when we walked, just before the murders happened. I remembered that my God is the God of love. Yes. I've taken a huge battering and sometimes I still feel very low. After praying last night, I realised that God is using this for a reason. He's given me hope for the future. I will not be alone."

Ruth leaned forward. "Naomi, you are amazing. Everything has been taken from you, yet you say this."

My joy was limited, however. Orpah was less convinced, although she meant well. "Did last night's prayers have any effect? Did your god strike down these murderers with a thunderbolt from heaven? I can't believe that you are not furious with these people and neither can my family. Whatever happened to an eye for an eye? Have you realised our lives are in tatters? What future are you seeing without your boys? Your God has already taken your husband. Naomi, I'm sorry but I still want to see justice done, and in time, I believe you will too."

"Fear and respect are not the same thing, Orpah, and neither are revenge and justice."

"I don't know what you mean, Naomi. It's beyond me. There's a score to be settled, whichever way I look at it. And you need to weigh up your own future. Urgently. This gang may not yet have finished dealing with immigrants." She stared ahead of her.

"Orpah, don't say such things. That's not the Orpah that Kilion was marrying. But you are right about my future. I think it's time I left Moab and returned to my homeland."

Part Two

"When Naomi heard in Moab that the LORD had come to the aid of his people by providing food for them, she and her daughters-in-law prepared to return home from there. With her two daughters-in-law she left the place where she had been living and set out on the road that would take them back to the land of Judah."

(Ruth 1 v 6-7, NIV)

Chapter Twenty-Two

Reality Bites

Ruth looked at me in amazement. "You are going back to Bethlehem?"

"Yes, Ruth."

I hadn't told them about Sara, so I decided to seek her out before lunch at the market and see what she wanted to say. I bade farewell to Ruth and Orpah and found Sara in the usual place.

After some pleasantries, and the information that she had known Orpah and Ruth's families since the girls were born, Sara started with some hard truths for me to take, prefaced by a deep and sincere apology.

She admitted that she had posed as my friend. Her husband had told her to do so, to open up a source of information about Eli. I asked her why, and she didn't know. She feared her husband, I think, or was I imposing my experience on an interpretation of what she said? I didn't know, but I understood why she had asked me endless questions, but what use could it have been to him?

None, I thought. Over many months, she had carried on

doing this, so it couldn't have been none. She told me she had wanted to be my friend, but he would not have allowed it. Next, I told her I had hidden when she had come round as the wedding plans were being finalised. What had she wanted? Her answer shocked me to the depths of my being. It seems there was a meeting in their house from which she, being a woman, was naturally excluded, but she overheard them discussing Eli's debts.

He'd run out of the kind of cash sums they had been taking from him. He had to be taken out, as they put it, as a statement to others who refused their demands.

Suddenly, Sara gathered her stuff and leapt to her feet. She garbled something about having spotted her husband in the distance, heading towards us. Danger, it seemed, abounded. I was to go one way, she the other. As we did so, she promised to speak soon to Ruth and Orpah, so they could pass on the rest of her discoveries. I was to say nothing.

That was my morning. Now, back in the house, I was having a normal conversation. Orpah was still taking the practical approach. "What about the food shortages in Bethlehem?"

It seemed so trivial, but I managed a reply. "A friend's husband was there recently. He says it's soon to be over. There's a good harvest coming."

Orpah didn't take this as I had. "There's plenty of food here in Moab. Stay here with us. We'll help you feel real again, the person you were before all this happened."

I needed to focus her on what I had decided. "I did get an answer to those prayers, Orpah. Food's not why I'm leaving. I'm being called to go home. Orpah, God's wanting me to return to Bethlehem."

Ruth smiled. "Your God keeps on giving! Naomi, I'm coming with you. There's nothing left for me here. I have to know more about this God of yours. He's really with you, isn't he? I'm not letting you go alone, and I'm not missing out on what he can teach me."

Orpah shrugged. "Me too, Ruth."

I shook my head. "I'm leaving next week. Please, both of you, stay here. You belong to Moab. You know people here. You've got friends and family."

Ruth was not of that mind. "I don't belong here. I will stick with you, Naomi. I'm convinced that your God will restore you and care for me."

Chapter Twenty-Three

Separate Ways

A week later, our journey to my home began. Orpah and Ruth had not mentioned Sara. I wondered if they had met. Maybe not, I thought, or they'd have told me by now.

I still walked well for a lady of a certain age. Ruth kept pace with me, but Orpah was a few yards behind. We paused occasionally to allow the younger woman to catch up. A nagging thought remained in my mind.

"We've been going an hour, ladies. It's not too late for you to change your mind. I'm worried that you've made the wrong move here. Why don't you each go home to your own mother?"

Ruth's response was immediate. "No. I am clear in my mind. You can, Orpah. I'm not speaking for you."

Orpah's tone revealed slight hesitancy. "No, I'm with you two."

I picked up the uncertainty but addressed them both. "Look, I know how it feels when your family is torn apart. I don't think doing that to your families is the best way to make up for what's happened to mine."

Orpah's demeanour became more pensive. "I hadn't thought of it that way, Naomi. And it's a forever decision, isn't it?"

As her mother-in-law, I needed to be compassionate. "Orpah, it's not too late. Go home, my love. Go and look after your own. Ruth, you too. Please."

Ruth put her foot down. "I'm sticking to my plan. But Orpah, maybe you could drop in on my family from time to time. I'd like that."

Orpah's mind was made up. "Do you mean it? Okay, I'm good with that. If I'm helping you, Ruth, then I'll go back."

The blessing I gave her was fulsome. "Orpah, your mum will be overjoyed if you go back home. I can promise you that. And your mum too, Ruth."

"Naomi, my future is with you. I've told you that."

"Ruth, you're a determined young lady who knows her own mind."

"I do. And it's telling me that I'm coming with you."

I pushed again. "Ruth, look, where I'm going, you'll be a stranger. You might be in danger. As we all know to our cost, there's little respect for those from other countries, especially recent war enemies. Go home, Ruth, please."

"No way. I feel a compulsion to accompany you, and I suspect your God may be behind it. It's not just for you, Naomi. My future lies in Bethlehem."

I laid out what I could offer her. Nothing. "What future? I'm an old lady. I'm a widow. I haven't got any other sons for you to meet and marry, and I'm not going to have any more, am I!"

Ruth took no notice. "You know when you said you'd been

praying, and told me your God is calling you back? Your face was so alive. Chemosh hasn't got a hope, literally."

I had a companion for my future. She would walk alongside me with the Lord, to Bethlehem and beyond. She would help me in the times I still felt low, wherever that was. I told her so. "I am putting all my trust in him for what I'm doing with you. I haven't felt purposeful for years, Ruth, and now, wonderfully, I do. That's why I know what I have to do."

Ruth had more to add. "After what you told me, I went home and tried to pray too. I don't know if your God could hear me, because I don't know much about him. What I do know, I like."

"Well, Ruth, as I've told you, he's the God of love. He will hear you when you pray. And he will answer your prayer."

She told me what I already knew. "Naomi, there's more. I have this overwhelming feeling that I should be with you. I can't explain it logically. It was a warm sensation which made me excited. I feel it stronger than ever right now. The Lord has confirmed me in my intentions."

I hugged her. "He has, Ruth."

I smiled at her friend. "Orpah, go home and do what you have promised. Let's all have a hug, and we'll go our separate ways."

Chapter Twenty-Four

A Coming Harvest

Six days later, with no bandits on any horizon, we sat down at the overnight shelter we'd found.

I was glad of the rest. "Not too far now, Ruth. We're doing well."

"Naomi, will you tell me something? What was Mahlon's dad really like? Mahlon was intrigued by him, but I'd like to know more. You haven't ever said much about him."

"He was a lovely man when we married. He cared deeply for his family. There were plenty of them for him to care about, as well as, eventually, the four of us. He kept in touch with them all. He had some land around Bethlehem, and they did too."

"Did he love your God?"

"Yes, Ruth. Especially before the boys were born. After that, he didn't always get things right, but none of us do, if we're honest. He could make a mess of stuff like the rest of us. But his heart was with God. Moab wasn't his best move, and he became more dependent on himself as the story evolved."

"Mahlon seemed a bit like that. Was he a chip off the old block?"

"You didn't get to know him too well. But yes, he was. He started well, knew the basics of his faith. Growing up, he blew hot and cold on it. He was slightly more tolerant than Elimelech and didn't like upsetting people. He improved on the first quality as he got older, and unchanged on the second."

"Was he a believer?"

"I'd love to say he was, but I can't. Mahlon set more store on what those around thought of him. He didn't want to be seen as a kind of religious nut like his mother."

Ruth smiled. "Is the wider family still in Bethlehem, even now?"

Naomi pointed towards the horizon. "We'll soon find out. It's the town you can see near the hill. See all those fields? They look ready for harvesting."

"And will your husband's family look out for you?"

"I don't know, Ruth. I'm just an old woman, a widow. That doesn't count for much in Bethlehem."

"Surely Elimelech's land will still be in the family, though."

"Yes. I'm hoping it might be mine to sell. Some of his family were very decent folk. We'll make contact with the relatives once we're settled. They'll need to know about his passing, of course."

"Will they still recognise you, Naomi?"

"Come on, Ruth, I'm only ten years older than when they last saw me! I haven't changed a bit!"

She laughed. "Do you think they might be a little bit surprised to see you back?"

"There'll probably be quite a few previous residents returning now the famine is over. And if the harvest is ready, they might be too busy to notice. I'm hoping they still have long memories in these parts, though, but they will recall Elimelech as a good man. They certainly don't know what happened to him."

"That will be such a shock for them to take as a family, coming out of the blue. Especially when they see you on your own."

An hour later, we were almost home. I had advice for my daughter-in-law. "Ruth, we're just coming into town now. Keep your head covered and ignore anything you hear. Stay close, my dear. You'll be safe with me."

My heart was flooded with joy as I remembered every inch of the town to which I had feared I would never return. Still, there was one question hanging over me. Had Ruth met with Sara? I was yet to find out.

Chapter Twenty-Five

A Long Haul

The next morning, Ruth caught me out. After so many years with the boys, I wasn't used to such pre-breakfast promptitude. "Ruth, you're up early! And after walking non-stop each day for a week. Why are you smiling?"

"I've got places to go. I'm going to get us some food."

"You can't! I love your keenness, but they don't know you from Adam. You'll be in danger."

"I'm not going out on the scrounge, Mum. I'm here to do my part. If your God is as real and as active as I suspect, He'll protect me. What are you doing this morning?"

"I'm speaking to the neighbours; I'm going to reconnect with the family. It won't be easy. I have some explaining to do."

"What kind of explaining? Why you went to Moab?"

"Sure. What happened to Elimelech. About Mahlon and Kilion, whom some of them never met. There'll be joy, anger and tears to deal with, and they won't all be mine." I managed a half-hearted laugh.

"Are you up to that? Are you really over all your pain? Are you sure?"

"It won't ever go away but it's less acute, Ruth. I need them to know what has gone on. I am convinced that the Lord wants them to know. There's a lot of catching up to be done. Ten years is a long time."

"They'll be interested to hear it all, Mum. I know they will. The good and the bad."

"It will be a long haul, Ruth, for both of us. In time, I'm going to tell them I was so low that I wanted to be called Mara, that word which means bitter. I hope I don't come across that way and they don't use that name for me, but I guess I deserve it. There are still dark moments when I'm back in that pit."

"Mum, you're bound to have those, but they'll remember you just as you were. They won't be changing your name. Listen, after I've got the food, I'll be off to find some work."

"Where, Ruth? You don't know anyone."

"It's obvious. In the harvest. There are always opportunities when its mad busy. I'll just use my wits until I find something."

"I'm praying that God keeps you safe, Ruth. Let's catch up this evening."

"Let me bring the food first, Mum! Then I'll be out of your hair."

Ruth was as good as her word. We sat down together as soon as she returned in the early evening.

"How was your first day, Mum? Do tell!"

"Amazing actually. I'd forgotten how well Elimelech was known in Bethlehem. Everyone I met wanted to talk."

"Did they take the news well?"

"With sadness, yes. Genuine sorrow."

"I hope it didn't reopen sores which had begun to heal, Mum."

"I still want to cry each time I tell the story because it hurts so much, especially when I get to Mahlon and Kilion. But there was a real warmth in the people. And some of them had seen us arrive last night."

"Your house has been left unoccupied for ten years. If it's like Moab, that's big news across the whole town when someone returns."

"They wanted to know who you were too."

"And what did you tell them?"

"The truth. I told them that you were the best daughter-in-law a mother could ever have."

"How did they take that, me being a foreigner?"

"They were surprised, to be fair. Some of them still remember the war. But the fact that you had come with me impressed them. They respected you for risking everything. I think they will accept you in time."

"Did you speak of your God with them? What did you say?"

"Not to all, Ruth. To those I trusted. I told them of Chemosh, and the killings, and how you were attracted to the Lord."

"Does that make me safer here?"

"Ruth, it has to be God at work. You are a figure of curiosity to them, for sure, and yes, safer is the word. Now how did you get on?"

"I walked a little around the fields and watched. There were some women who walked a few yards behind the men who were cutting the barley. They collected the bits they missed."

"We call that gleaning. It's a way of feeding the poor. What happened next?"

"I saw a group of harvesters who didn't have anyone doing that, so I asked the man in charge if I could pick up the remains. He said yes."

"Did you talk to them at all?"

"Not at first. I kept my head down. I didn't stop."

"So, you worked hard. Were they impressed?"

"Mum, I don't know. I didn't look at them. But then something amazing happened."

"And what was that?"

"The owner of the field we were in showed up. He asked the one in charge who I was. He didn't recognise me."

"And what did he say?"

"He said I worked hard. He told the owner my name, and where I came from. He mentioned you."

"Word travels fast round here! Did he throw you out?"

"No, the opposite. He gave me permission to stay. He told the others not to harm me."

"He sounds like a nice man, Ruth."

"It was so lovely the way he greeted his workers. He obviously cared for them all. That's his servants and the hired people. He wished them God's blessing."

"I don't suppose that kind of thing happened in Moab."

"No, I'm not sure Chemosh having a hand in your day would have been seen positively. Remember, he demanded human blood as a sacrifice. This was a bit different."

"Ah, yes. And then?"

"He told me I could have water to drink whenever I needed any. And then he astonished me."

"He astonished you? Men can seem astonishing and even caring if they are after something only a woman can provide, and I don't mean a decent dinner."

"It wasn't that. Not in the slightest. This man knew all about me. He said he knew I was a foreigner who had come to find security in the Lord. He told me I could live in Bethlehem under God's protection."

"Well, those wagging tongues have done well. Who is this man of God? Did you get a name?"

"I did. His name is Boaz. He then made sure I had a good lunch. And he's given me a sack of grain to bring home, so there's some for you. I couldn't eat all the lunch either, so there's some for you there too."

CHAPTER TWENTY-SIX

PARTY TIME

"Boaz? Did you say Boaz? No way! He belongs to the family! He's highly respected here – or at least he was before we left, and it sounds like he hasn't changed. Boaz is a good man."

"Mum, it all felt like it was meant to happen. Do you think it was a coincidence?"

"That's a good question, Ruth. It may be one you have to answer for yourself."

"I've got a few days to think about it. Boaz told me to stay with the workforce until the harvest is in."

"I'll make a few enquiries around town. I think he can help us more. He's got some legal rights which Elimelech used to speak of. Ruth, you've made an important connection."

"Have I done that, Mum, or is it the Lord?"

"Maybe the Lord is your connection, not Boaz. Who knows?"

Life in Bethlehem resumed the rhythm I recalled so well. Ruth was out most days. Then one particular day, she returned with a different demeanour. What was occurring?

I was soon to find out.

"We've been back for two weeks already, Ruth. Have you made friends yet?"

"I saw some of the girls in town this morning, the ones I worked with on the harvest. They say it's the night of the party."

"That's right. There's a tradition which the famine didn't take away. Boaz always hosts a celebration and thanksgiving for the workers once everything is done. Are you going?"

"I don't know if I dare, Mum. I'd like to. He really looked out for me."

"He has taken care of us, Ruth, not just you. He's made sure we've had plenty of food since the day you met him."

"He is such a kind man. He cares so much about other people."

"Ruth, speaking of how we look after others, I've been thinking. You have settled so well in Bethlehem. Everyone seems to admire you for what you have done for me in bringing me home."

"Mum, I learned something from you when we first met. You found it in your heart to love me, a Moabite girl. Even on the darkest of days, when we felt so sad, you managed to put Orpah and me first."

"Ruth, I know I thought it would take a long time, but the Lord's hand is on us. I think the moment has come to make you permanent around here. We need to find you a new husband. It's what Mahlon would want. You could start your own family."

"After all we have been through, it would need to be someone special. Otherwise, I'm staying with you."

"If you met someone who made you feel happy, safe and secure, would you marry him?"

"Maybe I would, but only once I knew you were okay. Does Boaz have a son? I'm sure he would be a wonderful boy."

"No. He doesn't. He has never married."

"I can't believe that. He's such a lovely man."

"Ruth, quite a lot of the younger men in the village have noticed you. I don't think it will be long before a proposal comes your way."

"But I'm a foreigner."

"It's amazing where a pretty face can get you, even these days. Just you wait and see. Men find you very attractive."

"To be honest, I'm very clear about the kind of man I want to marry, and most young men don't tick the boxes. With Mahlon, there was something different."

"Ruth, you do know your own mind! That's rare in one so young!"

"Mum, I've listened to your story. Don't think I haven't learned anything from it. There's more, though. Since I met you, I have felt a guiding hand on my shoulder. It's like a greater force. Meeting Mahlon was a prelude to a greater purpose. Will you help me move forward? I don't know how things are done round here. It's not me that knows my mind, but a greater, better power."

"It sounds like the Lord has reached down to you, my dear. Of course I'll help. We'll start by praying his blessing on us, and then we'll see where He prompts you."

"May I ask you a question about Boaz? Why didn't he ever marry? He'd have made a fine husband for one lucky girl."

"That's a good question. I suppose he's got a business to run. He employs people. Managing a workforce well is a lifestyle in itself."

"That shouldn't stop him marrying, surely."

"True. He was always decisive, though. He was also a man who knew his own mind. He didn't waste time in any aspect of life."

"What are you saying, Mum? That he simply didn't want to marry?"

"No, my love. He just didn't meet the right person. You knew immediately that Mahlon was right for you, didn't you?"

"Yes. At the time, he seemed so much more mature than the local boys I knew of. And he was a bit mysterious."

"My Mahlon? Mysterious? I've never heard him called that before!"

"At the moment I first met him, I knew he was the one for me. I was even more sure when he started speaking."

"Really? Kilion certainly underestimated his big brother! But that's such a precious feeling, and such a special moment. Unique."

"Unique? Almost, Mum. I've actually experienced that feeling twice."

"What? Did Mahlon know? What happened? Did the other boy not feel the same? He must have been mad to turn you down. Was that acceptable in Moab?"

"No. There was never anyone else."

"What on earth do you mean, then?"

"It wasn't even in Moab. It was on my first full day here. I thought it was impossible, but the experience has stayed with me. Is this the Lord's hand?"

"It might be. We need to test it carefully to work that out. I'm guessing it was one of the workers in the field with you. Which one?"

"None of them."

"Not the foreman? He's a servant. A good man, I'm told."

"Not him either."

"I can't imagine there were any other men around that day. Come on, let's stop this guessing game. Who are you talking about?"

"Mum, it was like when Mahlon spoke. I was entranced. I heard his greetings and his words of encouragement, and it was like being flooded with warmth and love. But he was way out of my league."

"I give up. I really do. Who was it? Do I know him?"

"Don't be shocked. It was Boaz. I knew it was meant to be. But I couldn't believe it could be him. I presumed he had a wife."

"Slow down, Ruth. Let's not be too hasty. Listen, if Boaz was willing, would you really be prepared to marry him? He's not in the first flush of youth."

"If the Lord is asking me to do this, it's a hundred times yes. But how could such a thing happen to me?"

"Ruth, my love, I don't know, but there might be a way. He's related to me. He's family. The fact that he's a bit older could work to our advantage."

"With the Lord, I'm not sure I need an advantage. Look, I won't care how old he is. When he's past working, I will still be young enough to take care of him. But will he want that? Isn't he a dyed-in-the-wool bachelor?"

"You are right. This won't be down to chance. Don't

misunderstand me, but he has certain rights now as an elder in the family. He may wish to exercise them. Let me do some checking."

"So do you think I should go to the party tonight?"

"I'm thinking that's a must. And let's see how well you scrub up!"

"A good scrub is what I need after all the gleaning I've been doing. I'll do it."

"It's not the ideal circumstances, but you've got three hours to look the best you ever did! I'm going to see what I can find out. We'll talk tactics early this evening!"

Chapter Twenty-Seven

The Foot of a Bed

Early evening came. "How good do you look, Ruth! Stunning!"

"Don't exaggerate, Mum. These clothes are all I have."

"I meant your smile. Listen. Foreigners can look mysterious, as you told me. We just need to ensure you get noticed."

"And what do I do when I get there? I'm going on my own, remember."

"That's your strongest suit, love. It wouldn't be good for him to find that you turned up escorted by one of the farmhands, for sure. When you arrive, keep a low profile and go and sit with the girls you worked with."

"Will there be food? Or should I eat some bread before I go?"

"That's an easy one. It's a harvest thanksgiving, Ruth, and Boaz will be sharing some of the fruits of the harvest with his workers – as a thanksgiving to them. Of course there'll be food. Lots of it!"

"And wine?"

"Look, we Bethlehem folk know how to have a good time, don't you worry. Music, dancing, food and wine – what more could you want?"

"Only for Boaz to notice me."

"I'm just coming to that. You'll need to show patience, my dear. Wait for your moment."

"And when might that be? I'm not sure I'll know."

"Let me teach you something, Ruth. If I've learned anything from life about men, it's this. If you want something, you should first see that they are well wined and dined."

"It sounds like that is taken care of. And is the Lord's hand still in it, with all this revelry?"

"Joy and peace come from him. Bin any remaining preconceptions of a Chemosh type fake deity. The Lord offers life."

"Wow, I haven't fully shaken off the culture I was brought up in, have I?"

"I'd be surprised if you had, my dear. It's one of the hardest tasks for those who come from the lies of false gods to discover the true one. The God of Israel rules with wisdom and love over everything He made. And that includes foreigners!"

"Sorry, Mother! Of course you are right."

"Listen, Ruth, I have more to tell you. Boaz will be on duty to some extent. He's the host. He won't be properly relaxed till everything is done and the party's over."

"So, I hang around till later, right?"

"You certainly do. He'll be crashing out on a makeshift bed in one of the barns tonight, when it's all over. Make sure you are the last to leave and let him bid you goodnight."

"Do I go home then? Is that it?"

"Absolutely not. Follow him at a respectful distance."

"Why? What am I going to do? I'm getting nervous about this."

"Here in Bethlehem, a girl lets a man know that she is interested in marriage by laying on the floor at the foot of his bed. It's a tradition. No words, just do that. Exactly as I told you."

"Won't he get the wrong idea? I don't think that's what the Lord would want, and me neither."

"With Boaz? Not at all. He's steeped in our culture. He'll know straight away what you mean. He'll respect you. And I think he'll be thrilled. Go, my daughter, go!"

"You know you didn't want to be called a new name? It's happened. You've got one. I call you Mum now. Have you noticed?"

"I love it, Ruth. That new name's wonderful. I'll see you tomorrow."

Chapter Twenty-Eight

Morning After

When morning revealed its dusty start to the day, my confirmed new daughter didn't make breakfast. When she arrived, I stopped her as she began her apology. "Never mind that. I've been awake all night! What happened?"

"I thought it wasn't going to work out."

"No! What went wrong?"

"Nothing exactly went wrong. It just didn't seem to be going right. I watched where he went to sleep, like you said."

"And then?"

"I lay down at the foot of his bed. More of an old straw mattress really, but I got the idea."

"Good girl. What did he say?"

"Well, he grunted twice and gave out a snore. He went straight back to sleep. Mum, he didn't know I was there."

"A snore? That's funny."

"Don't forget the two grunts!"

"I won't. So, what did you do?"

"I nearly gave up. I thought maybe the Lord was telling me

this was not going to happen. So, after a couple of hours of waiting, I lifted my head."

"And? You obviously didn't come home."

"No, that's what woke him up. And he was amazing."

"What did he say, my daughter?"

"He was astonished to find me there and willing to marry him. He said that there were lots of younger men available who were much better looking than him, and he didn't know why I had chosen him."

"Did he say something else?"

"Yes. He spoke of being a kinsman-redeemer. He said he wanted to do things properly. Mum, what's a kinsman-redeemer? I just nodded when he said it."

"Slow down, girl. Is he taking you up on the offer? Are you going to be his wife? Did he say yes?"

She repeated her question. "What's a kinsman-redeemer? I'll answer your other point when I know what one of them is. His answer hangs on this."

"I don't understand that, but okay. Boaz is family. The way it works here is that when a male family member dies, another one has the right to take action to stop the line from dying out. He's a kinsman-redeemer."

"That sounds a bit cold."

"Not at all. It often doesn't work out. When it works, it is amazing, because it is done in love."

"Good. Carry on, Mum."

"Well, I am selling the land held by Elimelech, so the family has first option on it. The fields come with strings attached."

"Strings? I don't like the sound of that. What kind of strings?"

"Fear not, my dear. If one of Elimelech's family buys the land, they have a duty to keep his family tree going. It's a kind of package deal."

"I get that. Forgive my self-interest, but where do I fit in?"

"I may be wrong, Ruth, but my guess is that Boaz has decided he wants to buy the land from me and marry you as part and parcel of the deal."

"What? Decision made? Marry me? Marry me? Wow. Deal? I don't know what to say. I'm speechless."

"No, you're not! You're babbling! Chill out, the Lord's hand is on this, I'm sure. It will happen if He so wishes."

"That's even more overwhelming. Wow!"

"There's one thing I haven't told you, Ruth. There is an expectation in all this that you'd have a child by Boaz."

"So, I should expect to expect?"

"I expect so."

"What's not to like in that? I'd have my own little family. Mum, I'd be really part of your family too. I couldn't be thought of as a foreigner anymore. I'd officially belong to you, and you to me."

"I don't need to remind you that you do anyway, my dear. What this would do is to enshrine it in law. Now before we get too carried away, am I right? Is Boaz going ahead?"

"He's not yet in a position to commit. He's got to check something out first. And it's not his bank balance."

"What is it, then? I can't imagine he's indecisive. He has always relied on the Lord, and this will be no exception."

"Let me put it this way. 24 hours ago, I had no idea what a kinsman-redeemer was, and now two of them have come along at once."

"Another one? Who is it? Does he have a name?"

"That's the funny thing. Yes and no. Boaz said it's your relative with a funny name."

"Oh yes. He's called Nonny. The nickname stuck. He was a rather cold fish, as I recall. A tad on the nerdy side, my husband used to say."

"Nerdy or not, it would seem that he could sabotage your plan. It lies in the way you all have to do things round here. This man could be an obstacle. He could stop Boaz in his tracks."

"How on earth could Nonny do that? He's a weather freak. He's not interested in anyone other than himself and his hobby. That's why he's still single."

"You might say that the outlook is not set fair. You'll remember this, I'm sure. This Nonny has priority over Boaz, in your law. Nonny could choose to be our kinsman-redeemer. If he exercises his legal option, there's nothing Boaz can do about it. He's going to find him later."

"How do you feel about that, Ruth? I'd like to tell you that every cloud has a silver lining, but Nonny would have his own opinion on that. Poor you, this is an awful situation."

"I'm keeping it out of my mind. If not, I'd feel sick at the prospect, to be honest. I have never clapped eyes on this man, and all this procedural tradition might mean I might have to marry him. I'm putting my trust in the Lord that it won't end with me feeling I ought to be heading back home to Moab."

"That won't be happening, Ruth. We are in this together and we need to pray."

"I have been doing that, Mum. Ever since Boaz put a doubt in my mind."

"Ruth, what we have to rely on is this. The Lord is a God

of love, and we are his children. Would a good father let this happen if it was bad?"

"No way. That's what doesn't match up for me. A loving father would never let this happen to his child, surely?"

"The Lord knows our needs, Ruth. I'm the last person to preach to you about this, but his ways are not ours. He prevails in the manner he sees fit, and all in his perfect time. He has you in His hand. I didn't understand all his ways during my years in Moab when I felt like a waste of space, but I now see I had to wait for you to come along. Ruth, the Lord is good."

"My hope is in him, Mum."

"Good. Like I told you, put the alternative totally out of your mind, not just at the back. My love, worry won't help anyone. Can you put all your trust in the Lord?"

"I am trying. It's easier to hope than it is to trust. Back in Moab, Orpah would be telling me this Nonny guy can't be allowed to block the pathway of real love. And I'd be hoping she was right."

"And someone would throw Chemosh into the mix. The difference between that evil spirit and the Lord is huge."

"I wish someone would throw Chemosh out of the window, never mind the mix. Could the Lord be testing me, Mum? Mahlon said he can do that."

"What do you think was going on with me back in your country, Ruth? The strength of my faith was examined to its very core. It's only looking back now that I can see what He was doing then."

"Would that help me?"

"Ruth, let's take a step back for a minute. We arrive in Bethlehem, me returning from a famine-avoidance absence and you a foreigner, from a country we were at war with 50 years ago. Correct?"

"That's right. The next day, I set off to find work. By chance I meet Boaz."

"Yes. You meet Boaz. Within a couple of weeks, we have a plan, so he notices you as a beautiful woman as well as a good worker. He learns your story and, it would appear, loves you for it."

"That's right. That works out too. Why do I feel now that it's all in jeopardy?"

"Mahlon used to say that there were lots of jobs there."

"In Jeopardy? Haha."

"Seriously, Ruth, deep down, do you think that any of what has occurred so far is by chance?"

"No, Mum, not when you put it that way. I don't. There's a plan being worked out here. But even the Lord's plans don't always end as we want, do they? I guess you didn't want to be widowed or lose your sons like you did."

"No, I didn't. But I did gain a wonderful daughter."

"But she turned round after we'd left Moab and went back home."

"Haha. You, you daft girl! I am talking about you!"

"I'll still be your daughter, whatever happens."

"That's right. God will bless us. Come on, let's go and pray together. Boaz will need some time to see how the land lies."

"As a farmer, he should be good at that. Anyway, I've agreed to meet him in town later in the day. The time's just going to drag."

"We'll pray together. Our God can give us a real sense of peace in the most trying of circumstances. Let's go."

Chapter Twenty-Nine

Consenting Elders

"Come on in, Ruth. I've had you in my head all day. You were right about how slowly the day would pass. Let's cut to the chase. Did you see Boaz?"

"Yes."

"Did he talk about marriage?"

"Yes."

"Did he say anything about the kinsman-redeemer business?"

"Yes."

"Had he spoken to Nonny?"

"Yes."

"Did he tell you what Nonny had decided?"

"Yes."

"Was it to buy my land?"

"Yes."

"Ruth, I'm so sorry. I thought this was the Lord's plan as well as a happily-ever-after ending. You must be devastated. Tell me what happened. How has it turned out like this? Tell me!"

"I will if you stop asking questions! Let me get a word in edgeways!"

"Was I doing that?"

"There you go again. Another question. Listen, Boaz spoke first to Nonny as he promised. He explained the situation and Nonny said he would buy the land. Boaz reported that he appeared to have quite a good business head on him. He has matured since his younger days and has broadened his interests beyond all things meteorological."

"That sounds promising. I expect he keeps contingency funds for a rainy day, though."

"Haha. He has been showered with opportunities. Increasing his land ownership portfolio is what he does these days. So, he said yes."

"That doesn't sound good, Ruth. Why are you still smiling?"

"Boaz explained that the land came with the responsibility for the surviving family of the deceased relative. He couldn't have the real estate without doing his duty."

"So, what did Nonny say?"

"Nonny backed off immediately. That would have financially compromised his own plans, if you follow me.

"That sounds promising."

"It was. Boaz had already told me he would do the kinsman-redeemer thing if Nonny didn't want to, and he would do it out of love. But there was still one more step."

"Don't tell me. That old thing involving a bunch of senior citizens by any chance?"

"That's the one. How do you know?"

"Don't forget I've seen it all before, when I lived here. The procedure is that the elders have to check out that everything is being done in accordance with the law before giving permission for the marriage to go ahead."

"That's exactly it. Boaz had to gain their consent. But they gave him more than he had bargained for."

"What do you mean?"

"Apparently, their approval was overwhelming. That's incredibly rare. Boaz was told that they, the elders, are looking forward to seeing our first child! They wished us every blessing."

"What did Boaz do?"

"Apparently, he went rather grey when they mentioned a child but soon got his colour back. He's now very enthusiastic."

"I'm not surprised! Once Nonny ruled himself out, it was the duty of Boaz to act as your kinsman-redeemer. But he'll enjoy the responsibility. He's got himself the loveliest and most beautiful girl in town! And at his age!"

"He's got the best mother-in-law too. He is redeeming both of us. Our futures are secure."

"I have something to tell you too, Ruth. God seems to have been speaking to me a lot lately. Your words confirm what I think he has been saying."

"Naomi, I don't see how the Lord could have blessed us any more than He has today. We are both taken care of. Forever. What more could He have given us?"

"Yes, I agree. God's love has flooded our hearts. But I feel that the Lord has put something else on my heart which I don't quite understand."

"Something else? Share it, please."

"He has laid it on my heart that Boaz's act of kinsman redemption is more significant than it is just to us. Don't ask me exactly how, I don't know. Around the time Boaz was speaking to you, I had a vision. It was that the blessing we have been given will extend beyond my own nation, and throughout the whole world."

"I belong to your nation anyway, Mum. I am not a stranger here, even though I come from Moab. Your people have embraced me and given me a home among them. I have been so fortunate."

"I would say that you belong to our God, Ruth, not our nation. One day, many more foreigners will follow in your footsteps. In fact, I know they will. The Lord is the God of all, not just the God of Israel."

"Mum, you know what, so much has changed since I went to that first Chemosh festival where I met Mahlon."

"God has brought so much good out of a bad situation, don't you think? It's amazing what He can do."

"Sure, for me, He's done wonders. But I'm thinking of all my friends back in Moab."

"Is that because they are still attracted by Chemosh?"

"Yeah, and tragically, they'll all be pretending to look forward to the next big appeasement. I seriously pray that they will come to know what I have found, although I wouldn't wish the terrible events which happened to us on them. They need to find the love, the power, and the truth of the Lord."

"You know what, He will have a plan for them, as He has a plan for us. You, Boaz, me – we will pray for Moab. But you, my girl, have a wedding to sort out."

"I do. And a family to raise! We've got some planning to do, Mum."

"We do. Not now, though, that's quite enough excitement for one day. We've got months ahead of us!"

"Up to the wedding and at least nine more after that!"

Chapter Thirty

Granny

"Where are you up to with the baby plans, Ruth?"

"Boaz is getting everything ready. He wants me to rest."

"That's not like a lot of men who just expect us women to get on with it."

"He is different, Naomi. He's thoughtful. He's wise. He's so caring."

"That is different. Very different. I wish my husband had been more like that."

"You've never really told me about him. I'd love to know more, if it's not going to pain you to tell me."

"My love, I'm going to be the granny to one of your children in the next few days. What do you want to know?"

"He loved you, didn't he?"

"Yes, he did. He loved the boys too."

"So where did he fail?"

"I'm not sure he failed. He just didn't get everything right."

"Forgive me saying this, but aren't you judging him in the

light of what you would have preferred him to do? Is that fair?"

"Thank you. I am sorry. You are correct to stop me. In which case, though, is 'fail' the right term?"

"It isn't. That also implies that we have a right to judge. This is getting quite heavy! Shall we just talk about how your views differed?"

"I wish everyone was like you, Ruth. We all love to weigh in with our judgement on other people."

"Forgetting that they look at us and do the same thing!"

"Yes! We're so good at spotting the faults of other people."

"It was the same in Moab."

"It's a human trait, I'm sure. What right do we have to do it? None."

"But it's so easy to fall into that trap. I just did, and I nearly took you with me."

"Okay. So how did we differ, Elimelech and me? First of all, when everything was going well here in Bethlehem, and the boys were very young, he was fine. He left me to look after them, of course, whilst he built up his business."

"I can't imagine Mahlon as a child. Was he like his father?"

"Both the boys were, well, typical boys. They were fun to bring up, and there were lots of laughs."

"Tell me about the laughs you had with your boys."

"When I taught them to play hide and seek. They loved the hiding part! Then it was my turn to hide, so I went and hid under the bed."

"What happened?"

"I thought it was a good place to hide because they didn't find me for a full twenty minutes. I was so pleased to relax, knowing they were busy searching."

"You didn't doze off, did you?"

"No, fortunately. But I did think they were quiet. I decided to give them ten more minutes to find me."

"And did they?"

"No. After half an hour I decided to tell them I'd won. I got up and went to tell them."

"Did they take the news well? Defeated by their mum?"

"They didn't take the news at all. They weren't there. It seems they got bored after ten minutes and went out to play with their friends."

"Ah. I'll have to watch out for that one when my family comes along!"

"You will. Ruth, you will need to correct your children when they go wrong. My way was gentle but firm."

"You say 'my' way. Was your husband not of the same opinion?"

"Oh yes, but he sometimes was distracted by other things and took what seemed to be to be the easy way out. He'd give in to them."

"That must have been tricky for you."

"It was. To make up for it, he tried to be over-firm when he did have the time. The result was confusion."

"They didn't know where they stood?"

"Precisely. Then I looked like the one who was always negative."

"That's tough. Did they ignore you, then?"

"No. Children won't do that if you're the one who feeds

them! Seriously, the older they became, the more they protected me. Especially Kilion."

"So did they begin to take after you or your husband?"

"Both, to be fair. Mahlon particularly developed plenty of self-confidence. Elimelech thought of him as a decision-maker."

"Was he wise, though? Elimelech, I mean."

"He always did what he thought was best."

"Oh dear. I take that as a 'no'."

"Ruth, none of us pray enough. We have the greatest source of wisdom ever in the Lord. I felt at times that Elimelech relied on his own thoughts too much."

"Was my Mahlon like that?"

"If I'm honest, I think you would have had a job reining him in at times. But in my case, it all came to a head when the famine broke out here."

At this point, Ruth held up a hand. Her question intrigued me. "That's why you all left for Moab, wasn't it?"

I replied anyway. "Yes. That was Elimelech's decision. They boys didn't want to go, and neither did I."

"Even though there were food shortages?"

"Ruth, the Lord has always provided for his people. To me it was about trusting in God. I thought we should have stayed."

"I'm glad you didn't. I would never have met you otherwise. Or found the Lord."

"You'll understand if I feel differently. At a simple level, that decision of Elimelech cost me his own life and that of my two sons, never mind ten years of trauma, despair, guilt and suffering."

Her expression was still one of puzzlement. I had to ask. "Do you know something I don't, Ruth?"

"Yes. Sara spoke to me, as you may know. Her information is quite telling. Her opinion of men as leaders has changed radically, if I can put it that way. You'll need to be strong, Mum, if I tell you what she recounted to me before we left Moab. I've been waiting for the right moment."

Chapter Thirty-One

Revelation

"Why, Ruth? Sara was my only friend there. What could she tell me that could be so shocking?"

"Mum, she wasn't your friend at first. Nor was she until much later. She was planted."

"Sara? Planted? Never!"

"I'm afraid so. Her husband liked to live it up, fine house, gourmet food, luxury in all things. Farming the land doesn't come with that kind of lifestyle. So he turned to crime."

I could not believe what I was hearing. "And Sara knew?"

"No, Mum, she didn't. She was managed and manipulated by her husband. Rumours of the famine across the border had spread. He heard that the rich would seek shelter in Moab. So, he got together with some like-minded acquaintances from the towns in our region. Sara said that some of them said it was revenge for the war, but most were motivated by evil."

"Chemosh?" My question was brief.

"They hid behind the name, certainly. It gave their dirty and disgusting aims a degree of plausibility, even a semblance of dignity. They set up a Chemosh-themed property management agency in each town, with a sister operation in Bethlehem. No Chemosh there, of course."

"Sara was told that much, I guess?"

"She was. She swallowed the story and presumed it was all respectable."

"What was it, if they didn't sell and let houses?"

"It's best described as people-trafficking. Done for outrageous sums. In the source location, Bethlehem, they enticed the wealthy with a promise of a fancy house in a land flowing with milk and honey."

"That's what my nation called our own promised land. You are telling me Elimelech was conned, aren't you?"

"I'm afraid so. He fitted the right profile. More money than common sense, with a measure of gullibility thrown in. He wasn't alone."

"No, he told me others would be journeying with us to Moab. We were alone, with a man the boys called 'Hood'. He kept his head covered, even in the greatest heat of each day."

"Elimelech was tricked. You were always going alone. Others left Bethlehem, but they were taken to other towns in Moab. The property management agencies had only one house in each town. Contact between fellow victims was not allowed."

"Were they not more susceptible to bandit attacks in such small numbers?"

"That was taken care of. The robbers were well known to the traffickers and agreed a fee. At some point on the journey, a payment would be made in respect of safe passage. It worked. There is still honour among thieves."

"Did she tell you why Hood went ahead of us into the

town, leaving us for a day on the other side if the border?"

"I assume that's to do with the house. They only had access to the one. The luxurious villas never existed. Hood went to clear out the occupants. A couple of others would have met him there. That's where Chemosh came in."

"Chemosh? I hope no human sacrifice was involved."

"It was simpler than that, Mum. Elimelech was a better bet, financially. They esteemed him to be richer. The occupants were taken out. Their stuff was dumped."

"Taken out, Ruth?"

"Murdered. They claimed the sacrifice was demanded by you know who. No-one could touch them for it."

"How was Sara not my friend? She spent a lot of time with me."

"That was complicated. Initially, you were being tapped for information about yourselves and your family. Then it was other suitable targets in Bethlehem. Neighbours, perhaps, or friends? Her husband interrogated her regularly on what she knew and fed the information back to his colleagues."

"And she never knew how the information was used?"

"No. Not until they got lazy. Before that, they charged Elimelech more and more for protection, for rent, for breathing their air, and he kept on paying."

"Ruth, by this time, he was sure the family was accepted by the townspeople. He told the boys to earn respect through hard work. He took on responsibilities himself, and his pay went up. Or so he said."

"It's true. But the more he earned, the more they demanded. Chemosh-backed death threats are a powerful incentive to pay. The boys were a problem, though. They were a hit with the local youth. They worked their way into acceptance. And then Elimelech stopped paying."

"That's a death sentence, if your information is right?"

"Normally, yes, but a high-profile murder of a sick man would not have gone down well with the community, who had taken a shine to the boys. His illness was the solution. Sara told me he didn't die from it."

"It was from poisoning, wasn't it?"

"How did you know, Mum?"

"She thought it was a remedy. She'd been tricked again. I gave it to my husband. So how did they become lax, this gang?"

"There was a meeting in Hood's house. Sara was sent to a back room, but the door had been left ajar. She heard him discussing your two boys, no more than that. She put two and two together and began to realise how Hood was earning the living from which her lifestyle had come. She was horrified."

"So, what did she do?"

"She decided to become the friend you thought she was. She tried to warn you something might be afoot, but first time, Hood appeared on the horizon at the wrong moment. Eventually, she summoned up all her courage and went to your house. She went twice but received no reply. At that point, she resolved to tell me instead."

I went very pale. Why hadn't I answered her knock?

Ruth understood my mindset. "If she'd known they were going to kill Mahlon and Kilion, she'd have broken the door down to tell you. Sara's a decent woman. She saw it as a vague threat at that point, Mum."

I still felt uneasy if not a little sick. Ruth shook her head.

"It might well have been that they'd got new victims for the house. They thought your family money had run out."

"So why didn't they target me, Ruth?"

"Maybe they did, and you inadvertently left the scene. Was your Lord protecting you for his purposes? That wouldn't surprise me."

"Why did they run away, if they were supposedly working out the will of Chemosh?"

"Eli's death appeared to be from his illness. Nothing too strange there. But the community back there aren't totally stupid. The wedding murders, the so-called sacrifices, would have frightened them. They panicked when you weren't there. That's the main reason why they fled."

"Was there another?"

"Yes. Sara was subjected to interrogation by her husband. He knew that she had rumbled him and his criminal way of life. If you were still at liberty, the whole enterprise was at stake. Right across the region. You, a foreigner, speaking out, put everything at risk. It would have been the end. He was on Eli's case from the start, in Bethlehem."

"What? Before we left?"

"Yes. He ran the whole show. Think back. The sad excuse for a camel, paying off the bandits, killing the previous occupants of your house, the tricking of his wife, organising the graffiti and other threats, then the blackmail, the poisoning of Elimelech and the stabbing of Mahlon and Kilion. The whole lot. And a whole lot more too."

Ruth hugged me. Relief mingled with tears at our stupidity. After a while, I felt I would be given the strength to deal with my remorse. Not quite yet, but soon.

My daughter-in-law smiled sadly. "I'm not much of a consolation to you, Mum."

"Ruth, you are my joy. We have to see all this in terms of God's plan, not ours. It doesn't make it hurt any less. You said there was more to tell, though. Let's finish this sorry tale."

"Sara understood early on that your life was being carefully managed. She then discovered that she was unwittingly part of that. What she didn't know till the murders was that her own life was being controlled just like yours, terribly so. She's back with her own family, feeling battered and bruised, but safe. Her husband won't be returning anytime soon."

"Good. Is that it?"

"Wonderfully, she has already started to tell your story in the town. She tells how religion was hijacked by evil men, and so many people fell for it. She says that from now on, men and women must work together in transparent relationships for family and leadership. Opinion is turning, Mum. The account of what happened to you must be repeated to the generations to come. But there's something terrible I still haven't told you."

At this point, Ruth took a deep breath. "Naomi, shall I go on?"

I nodded but made no eye contact. What she had to relate next took my breath away.

"Sara told me that something odd occurred. Her husband seemed to have a total change of heart."

"You mean he repented? That's good, surely." I sounded unsure and found my head was shaking with negative expectation.

She avoided the issue. "Well, he gave her the phial of

medication for Elimelech. She was relieved, if slightly incredulous. Kindness after all these years."

"I'd have been stunned. Shame the medication didn't work after such a turnaround."

"It did, I'm afraid. Tragically, she'd been conned. Eli's death was a total shock for her. The phial contained a deadly poison."

I gasped. In the multitude of twists in my tortured mind, there came a strand of relief that at least it hadn't been me that had killed him. Then the inner hammer blow struck. It was me who had administered the death phial, albeit in innocence.

I was immediately back in my world which could go no darker than the black I'd been in. It seemed I was destined to remain there forever. I burbled something to Ruth, telling her that I should have tried to love Eli more but had let him down. Right then, I wished it was I who had taken the poison. If there'd been a second phial, I would gladly have had that too.

Ruth held me closely as I told her all this. She was gentle, empathising and speaking words of hope. She told me that my suffering was a result of Eli's controlling behaviour, and through my darkness, I began to believe it. This time, it felt like I was not alone.

She squeezed my hand as a first contortion crossed my daughter-in-law's face. She kissed me. "Look, I'm going to have to go home now, the pains are coming."

I couldn't leave her. "I'll walk with you. We'll take it steady. You'll be fine. I'll see you home and leave you in the care of Boaz. I wish Sara would find out about him. He values you properly, puts you first, and keeps the Lord in the marriage relationship."

Ruth took my arm, and we set off steadily.

The new day brought hope afresh, although my inner tussles had dissipated only slightly. I called at the house. "Ruth, are you there? Is everything well? I've just seen Boaz walking down the road, but he was so distracted that he didn't even see me."

"Mum, come in! It's a boy! Do come and hold him. He's just perfect! Boaz has just gone for some food. He's had no sleep whatsoever."

"No wonder he blanked me then! Poor man, just think what he's gone through! Only joking, love. One thing will change for him, forever."

"And what's that?"

"His definition of a good night. Before he met you, it probably involved a banquet fit for a king, lots of wine, maybe music and dancing."

"And now?"

"My dear, he will delight in unbroken sleep."

"Thank you, Granny! Now my baby needs a cuddle!"

"From me? Me hold your child in my arms? I never thought I would do this. The Lord has truly blessed me."

"Why are you crying, Mum?"

"These are tears of the greatest joy I have known for many a long year."

"Mara's gone forever, then?"

"She has. The bitter woman will never come back."

"She didn't last too long then!"

"Names can be ephemeral, my daughter. What are you going to call this gorgeous boy?"

"Boaz and I talked through everything you told me yesterday. We are naming him Obed."

"I think I know why."

"Boaz chose it. It means 'servant', or 'worshipper'."

"May the Lord bless the three of you. And do one thing for me as your married life continues."

"I will be an obedient daughter. I'll do exactly as you say, Mum."

"Good girl. Just remember always that Boaz loves you – but he's human too, like Elimelech. Promise me that you'll hold to the truth of the Lord and you'll be fine."

Postscript

"The women said to Naomi: "Praise be to the Lord, who this day has not left you without a guardian-redeemer. May he become famous throughout Israel! He will renew your life and sustain you in your old age. For your daughter-in-law, who loves you and who is better to you than seven sons, has given him birth."

Then Naomi took the child in her arms and cared for him. The women living there said, "Naomi has a son!" And they named him Obed. He was the father of Jesse, the father of David."

Ruth 4, vv 14-17, NIV)

Gratitude

This book has only been made possible by a group of people who have been unstinting in their support and encouragement. Hilary Skinner, Jane and Laurence Bozier, Rev. Lyndon Perry and his brother Steve, Dr. Phil Johnson and Dr. Paul Cooke (of France Mission) have all contributed generously to the editing and production process.

My dear friend Lucy Christian has brought her unique artistic flair to the cover artwork, based on an idea by a young artist of similar talent, Amy Peacock. Amy's brother Mike's role as a sounding board has been equally appreciated over many months.

Finally, and most significantly, I thank the Lord for the original plot. Without Him, none of this would have been possible!

John Adamson
June 2025

Printed in Great Britain
by Amazon